DREAM DOODLE DRAW!
Make-Believe Magic

Sweet Treats • **Dress-Up Time** • **Grow, Garden, Grow**

LITTLE SIMON
New York London Toronto Sydney New Delhi

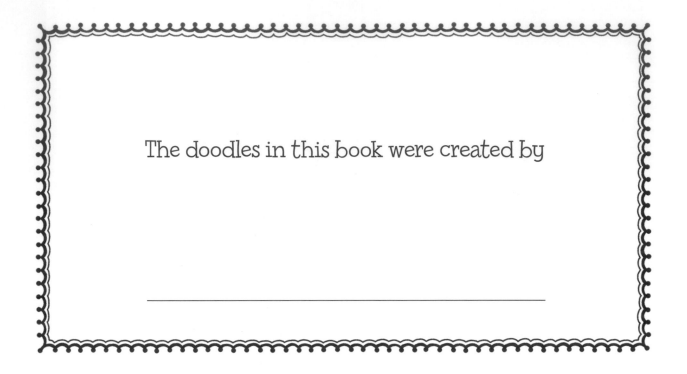

The doodles in this book were created by

_____

LITTLE SIMON

An imprint of Simon & Schuster Children's Publishing Division

1230 Avenue of the Americas, New York, New York 10020

First Little Simon bind-up edition May 2016

Sweet Treats copyright © 2014 by Simon & Schuster, Inc.

Dress-Up Time and *Grow, Garden, Grow* copyright © 2015 by Simon & Schuster, Inc.

For information about special discounts for bulk purchases, please contact Simon & Schuster Special Sales

at 1-866-506-1949 or business@simonandschuster.com.

The Simon & Schuster Speakers Bureau can bring authors to your live event. For more information or to book an event contact the

Simon & Schuster Speakers Bureau at 1-866-248-3049 or visit our website at www.simonspeakers.com.

Designed by Jay Colvin

Manufactured in China 0816 SCP

2 4 6 8 10 9 7 5 3

ISBN 978-1-4814-6291-4

The contents in this book were previously published individually as *Sweet Treats*,

Dress-Up Time, and *Grow, Garden, Grow*.

Who is ready to bake? Color in this bakery scene,
and let's get started!

Decorate these cupcakes!
What flavor are they? Write the flavors on the lines below.

These doughnuts need some sprinkles!

What's baking inside this oven? Draw it!

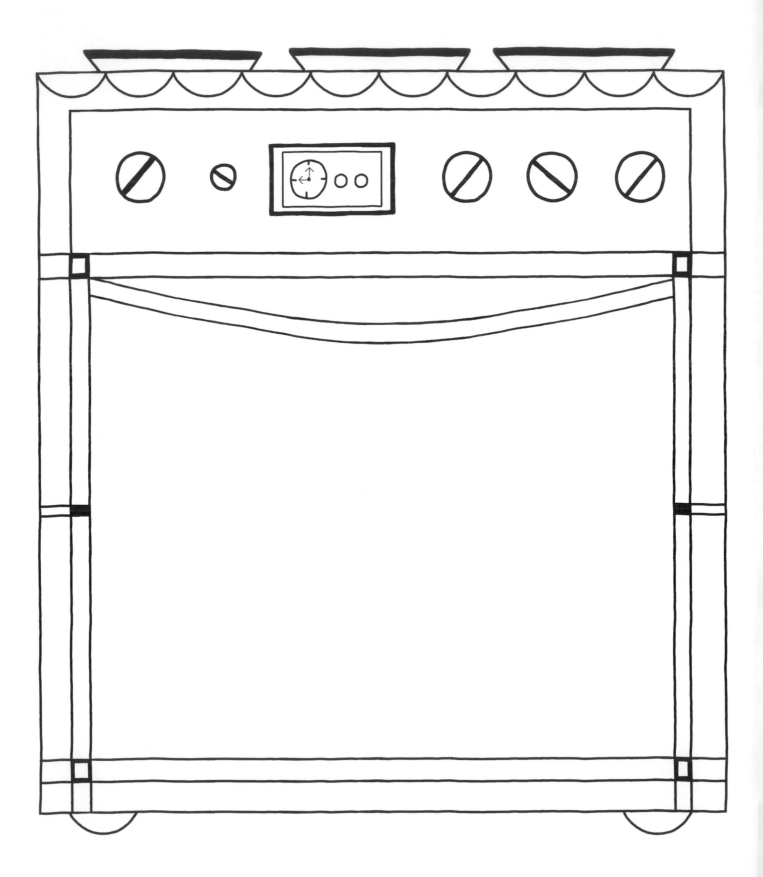

What's cooling on the counter? Draw it!

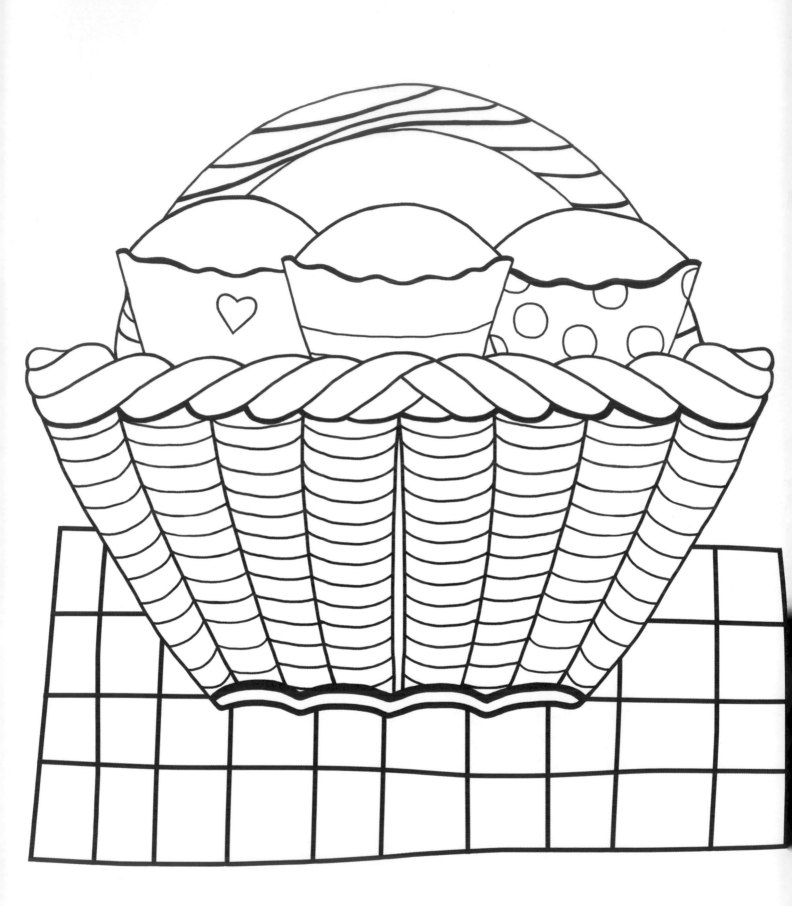

It looks like someone is having a picnic!
What kind of muffins are in the basket?

Draw a delicious treat on the plate next to this glass of milk.

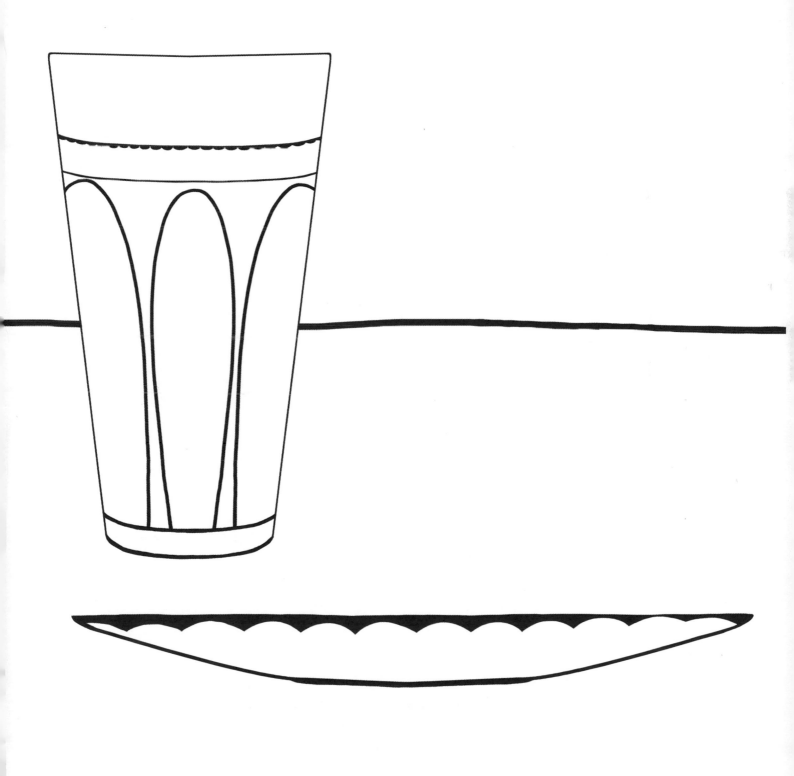

Put your favorite candy toppings on this ice cream!

Put your favorite fruit toppings on *this* ice cream!

Draw polka dots and stripes on the cupcake wrappers.

These cookies need some decoration!

Write something special on this cake.

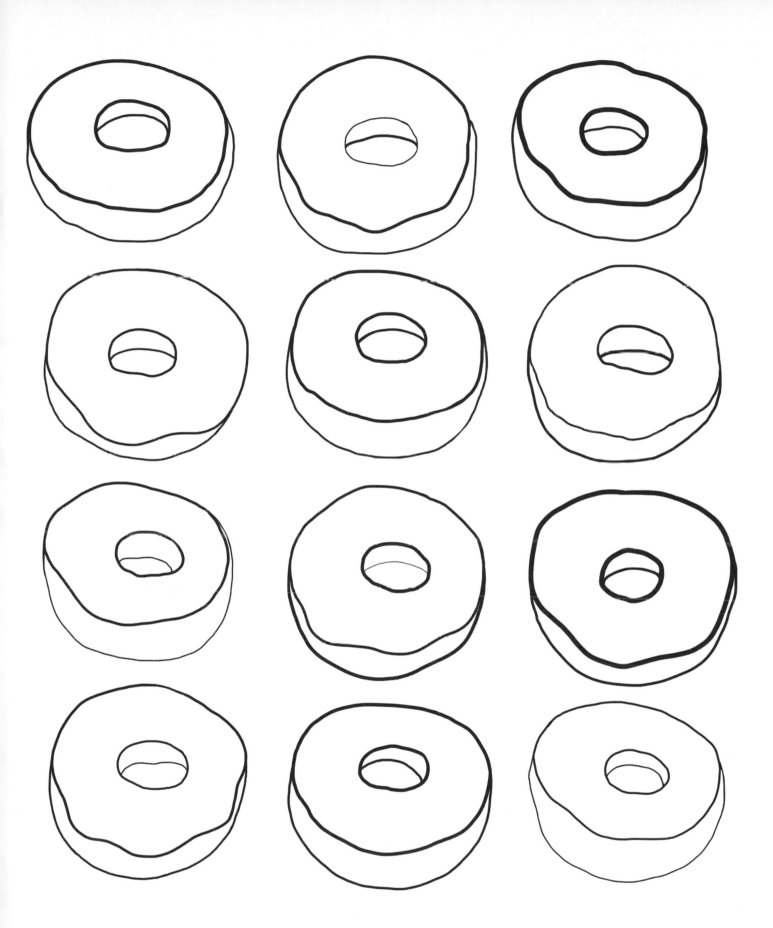

These doughnuts need to be decorated for a party!

Add your favorite treat to this page.

This cake just came out of the oven.

What flavor is each layer? Color the layers!

Whose birthday is it? Decorate the room with streamers and confetti, and add some people if you want!

Now decorate the cake!

Draw smiley faces on these cookies.

Doodle some patterns on these yummy cakes!

These cupcakes need something more—can you frost and decorate them?

Fill this page with sweet treats!

Connect the dots to see an icy surprise!

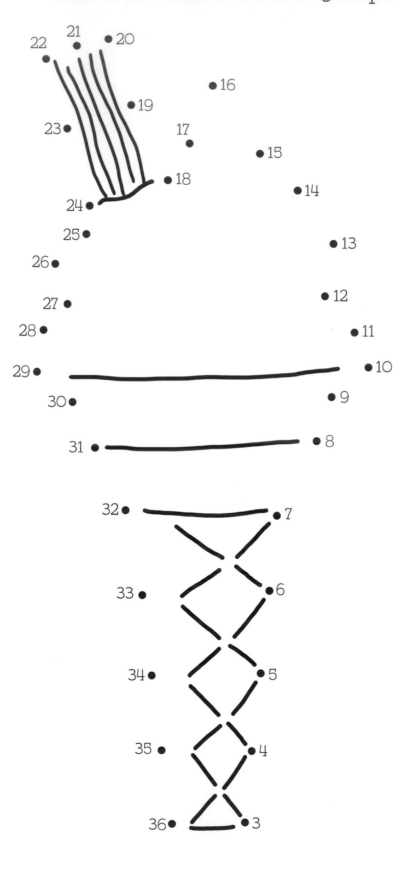

This bakery makes lots of delicious treats!

Looking at the ingredients, can you guess what kind of bread this is?

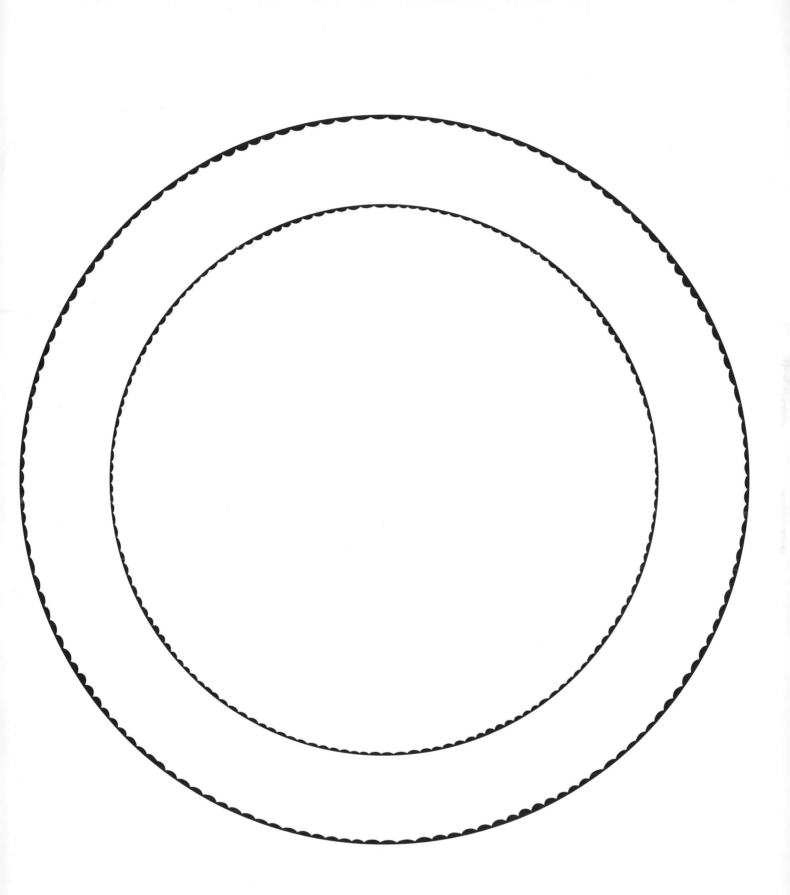

Add your favorite treat to this plate.

These cookies need to get to the oven!

Start

Can you help them find their way?

Finish

Looking at the ingredients, can you guess
what kind of cookies these are?

What's baking inside this oven? Draw it!

What's cooling on the counter? Draw it!

Use the shapes and patterns on this page
to decorate the cake on the next page.

Ice these cookies with your favorite colors.

Color in these sweet treats!

Draw the other half of this cupcake!

Color in these jars of candy.

And add some candy to the bottom jars!

This banana split needs some color!

Color in the cookies and hot chocolate.
Then doodle a cool design on the mug!

Give these doughnuts some sprinkles.

Color in these yummy ice pops!

Connect the dots to see a fruity surprise!

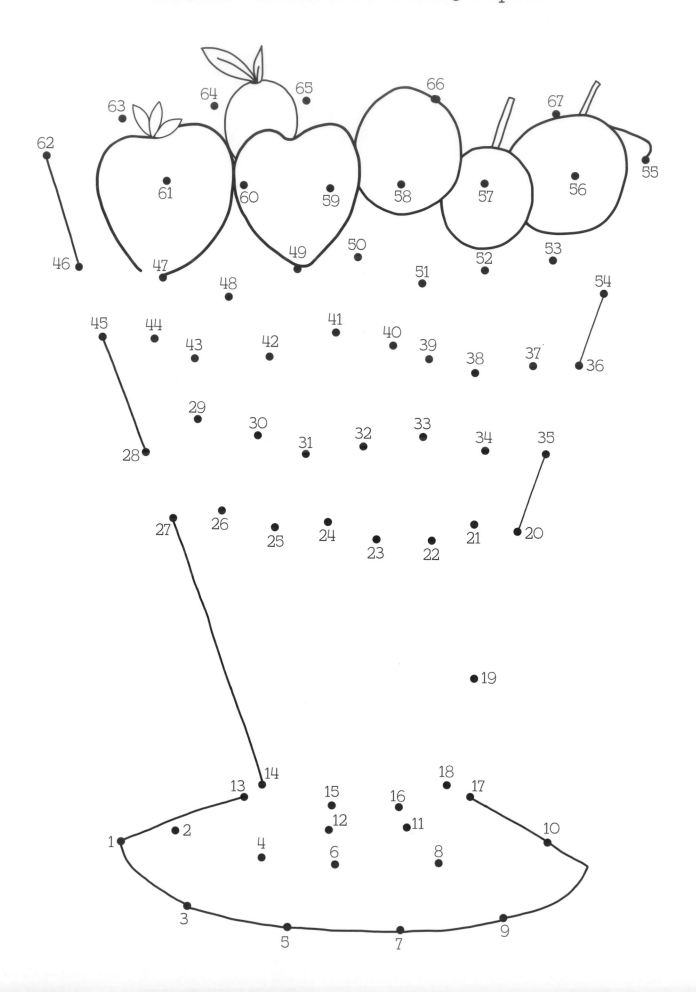

Decorate these aprons.

Draw some more doughnuts on this page!

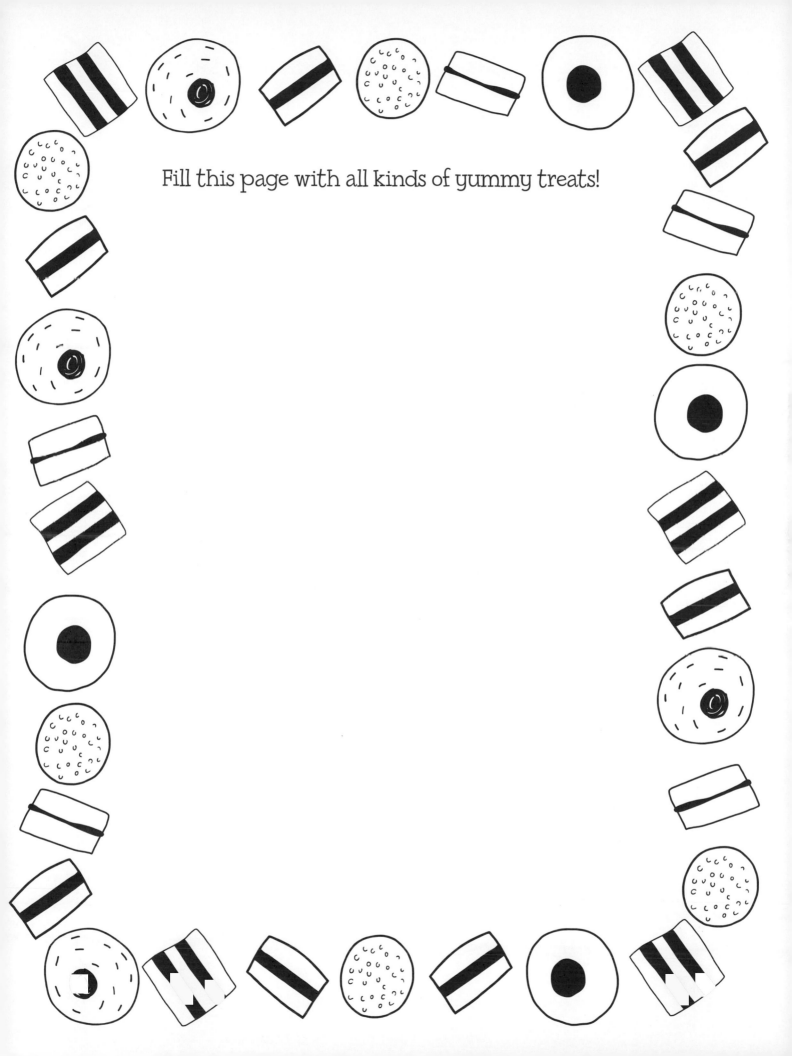

Fill this page with all kinds of yummy treats!

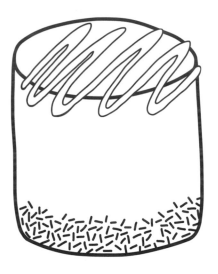

Color in these treats!

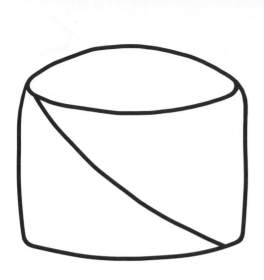

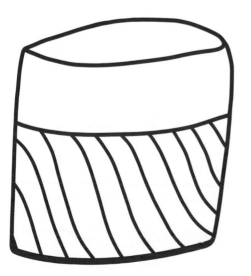

These ingredients are for the treat on the next page.
Color them in.

Yum! Now color the fruit tart.

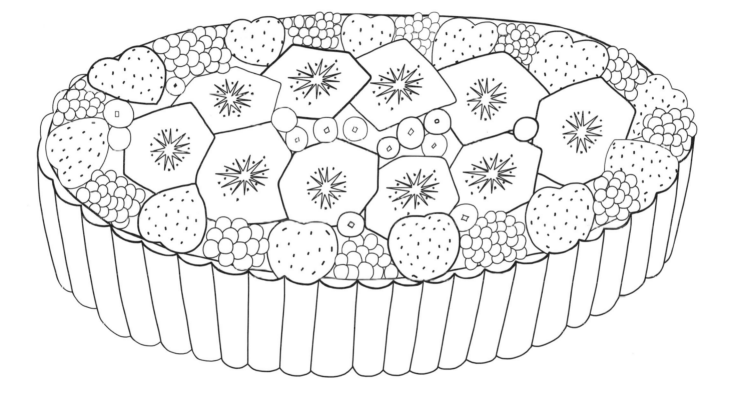

Finish decorating this birthday cake for your best friend!

Color in these lollipops.

Can you spot these images in the scene? Color them in!

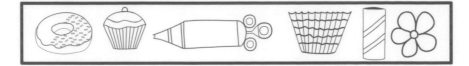

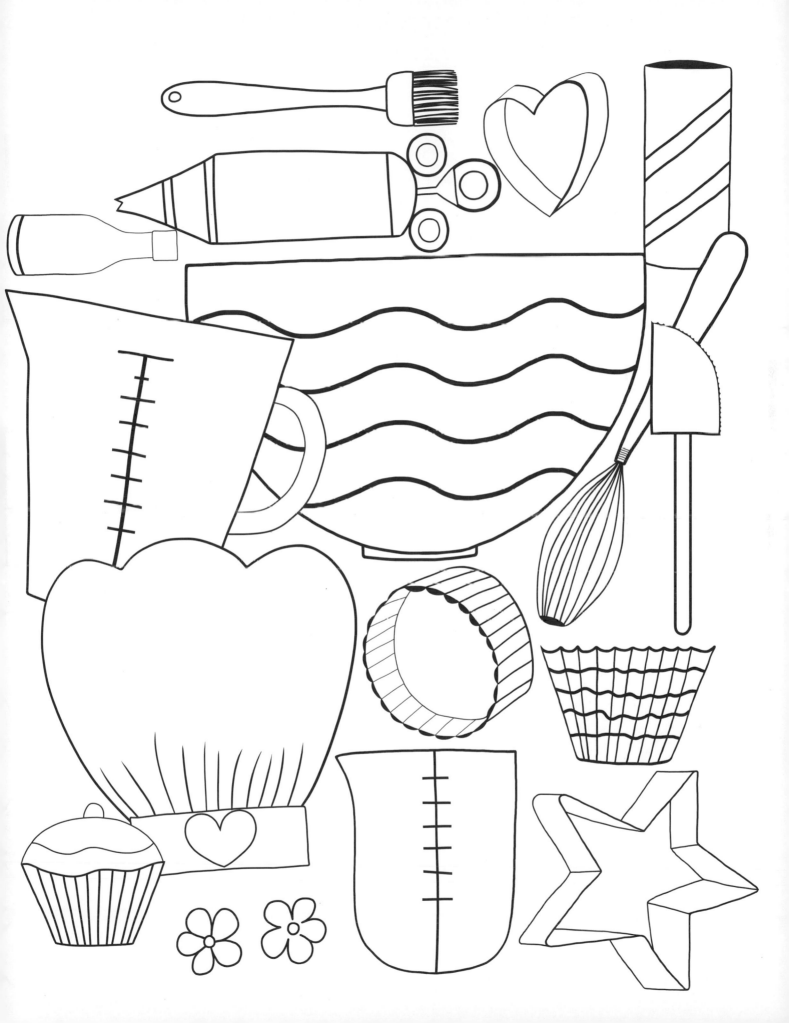

Write something special on the top of this cake.

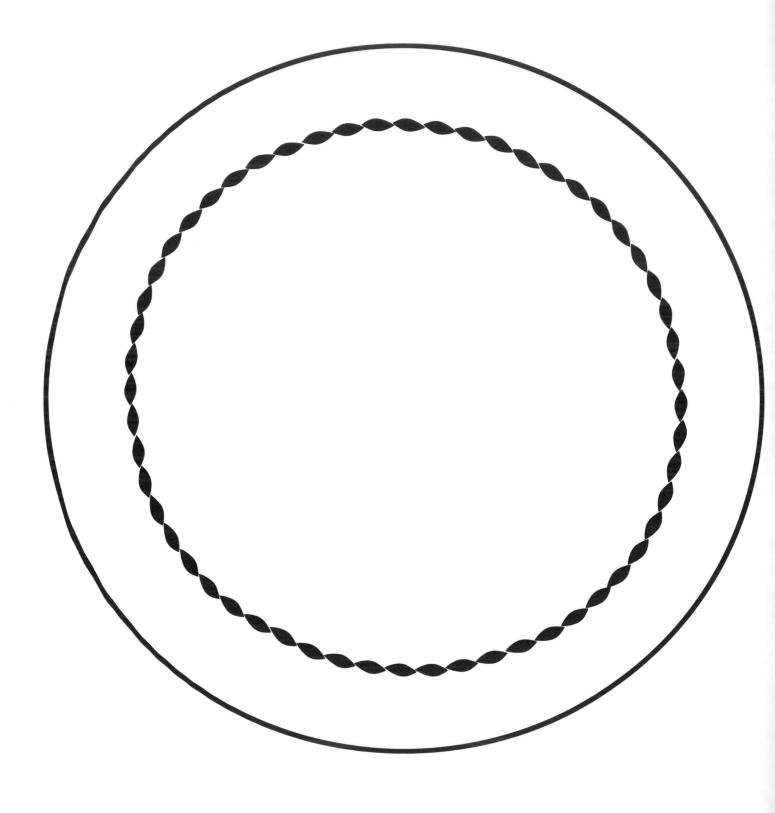

This chef is trying to figure out what to make.
Help him decide by drawing it in his thought bubble!

Hey! Who took bites of those doughnuts?

Draw your own doughnuts!

Can you decorate the cake with the items below?

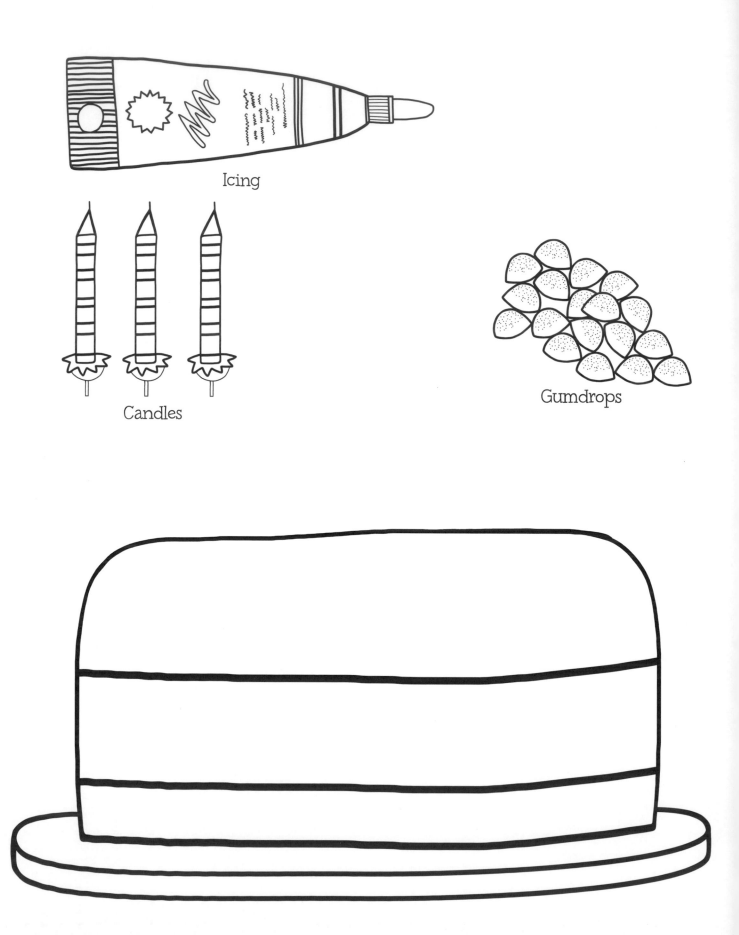

Icing

Candles

Gumdrops

This cake just came out of the oven.
What flavor is each layer? Color the layers!

Add your favorite treat to this plate.

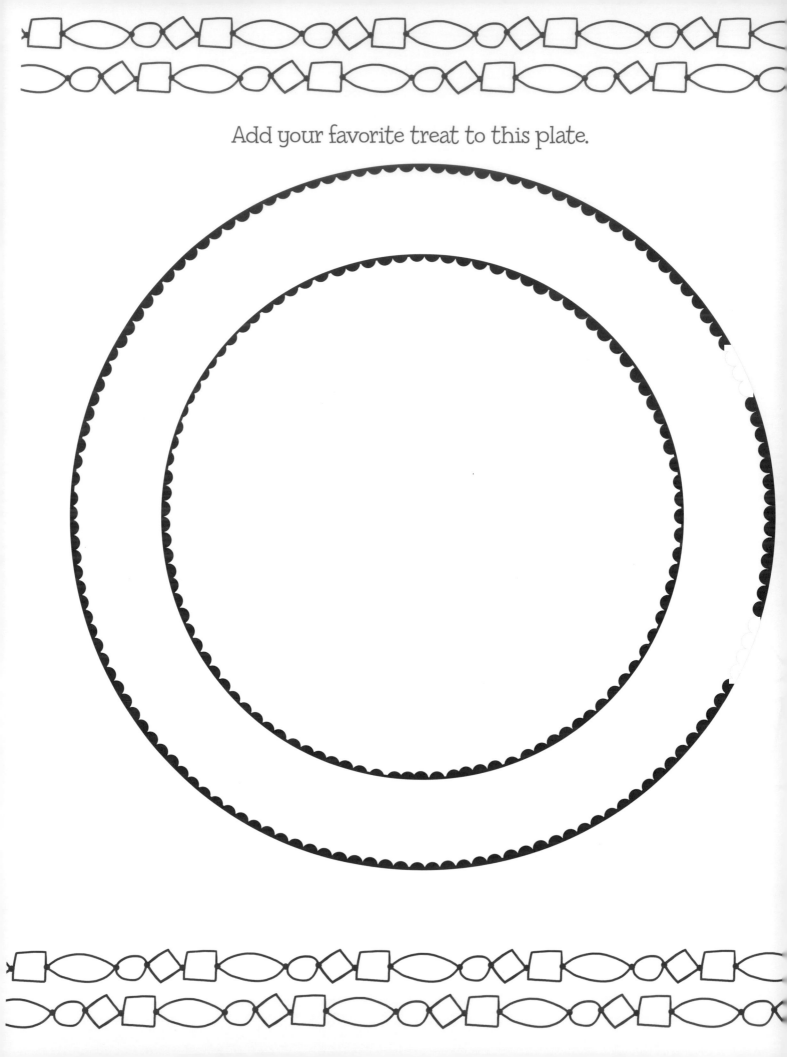

Color in these delicious milk shakes!

These ingredients need to get to the mixing bowl!

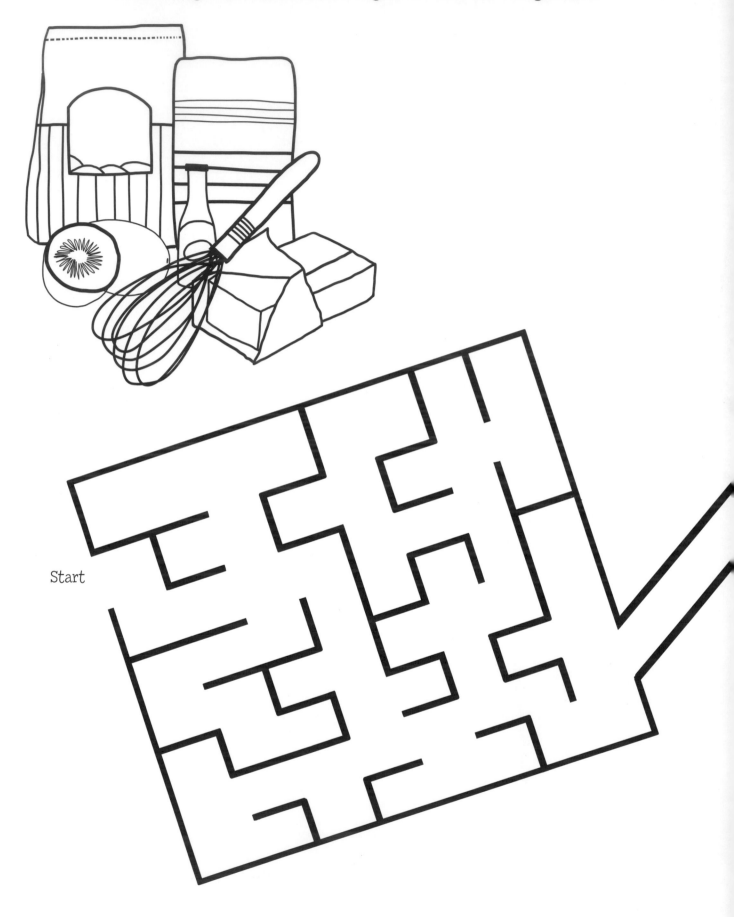

Start

Can you help them find their way?

Finish

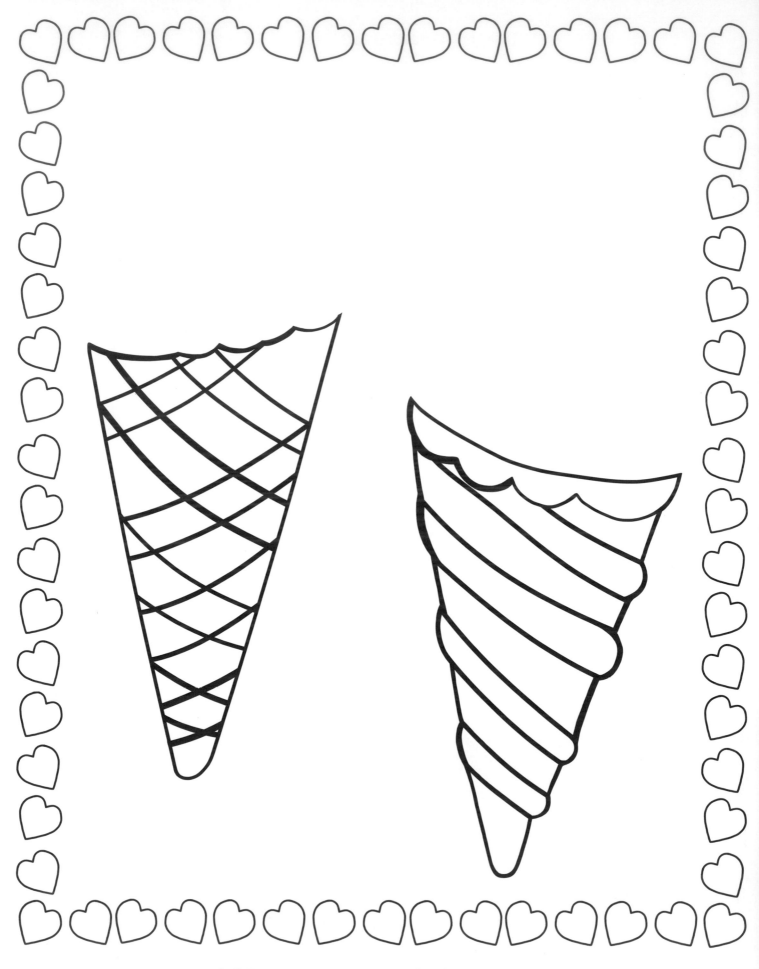

Add some ice cream to these cones!

Draw some more candy on this page.

Hey! Whose hand is that in the cookie jar?

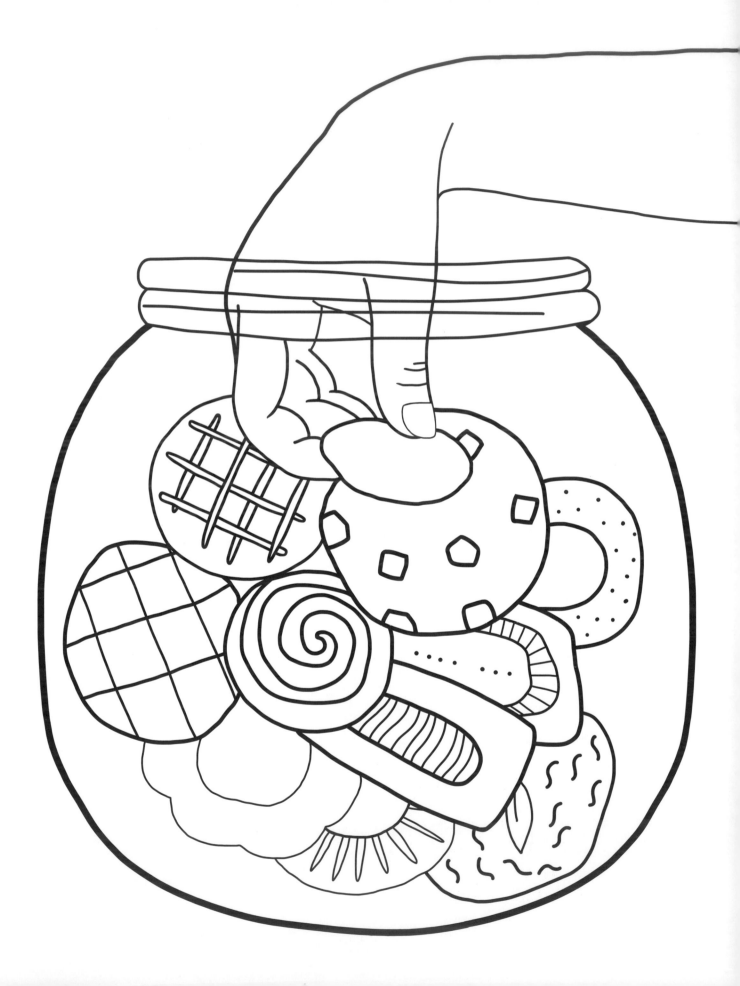

How old are you? Finish decorating this birthday cake
and add the right number of candles.

Looking at the ingredients,
can you guess what kind of muffins are on the next page?

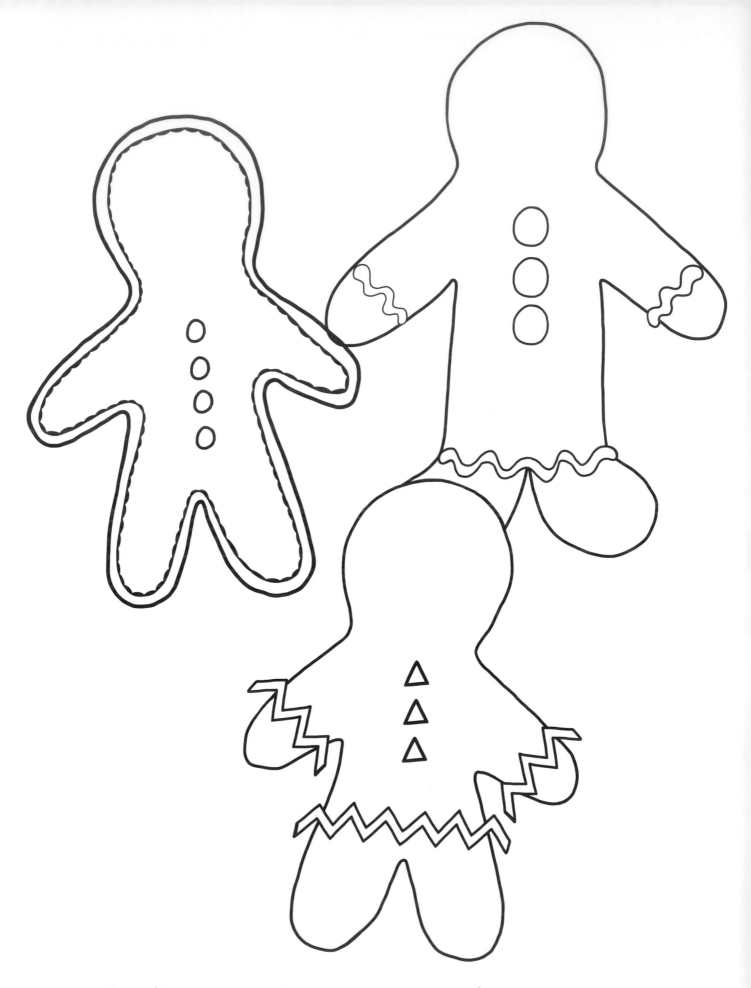

Give these gingerbread cookies some faces and clothes!

Draw the other half of this cake. Then color it in!

Yum! Candy bags!

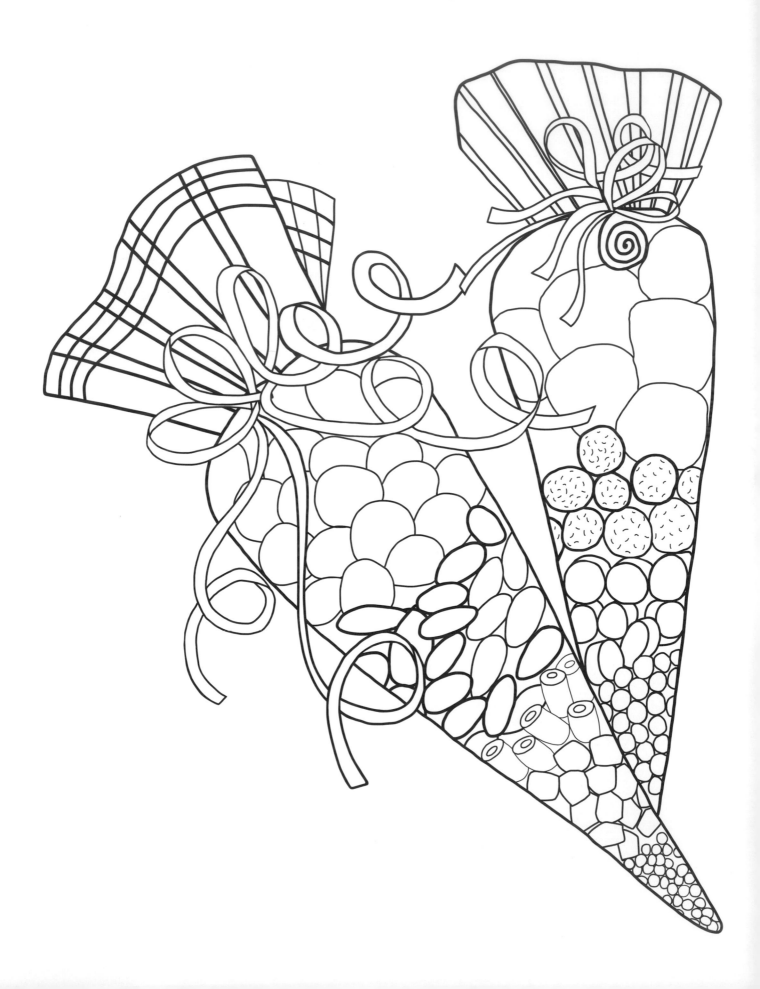

Color in these pretty pies.

Put your favorite toppings on this ice cream!

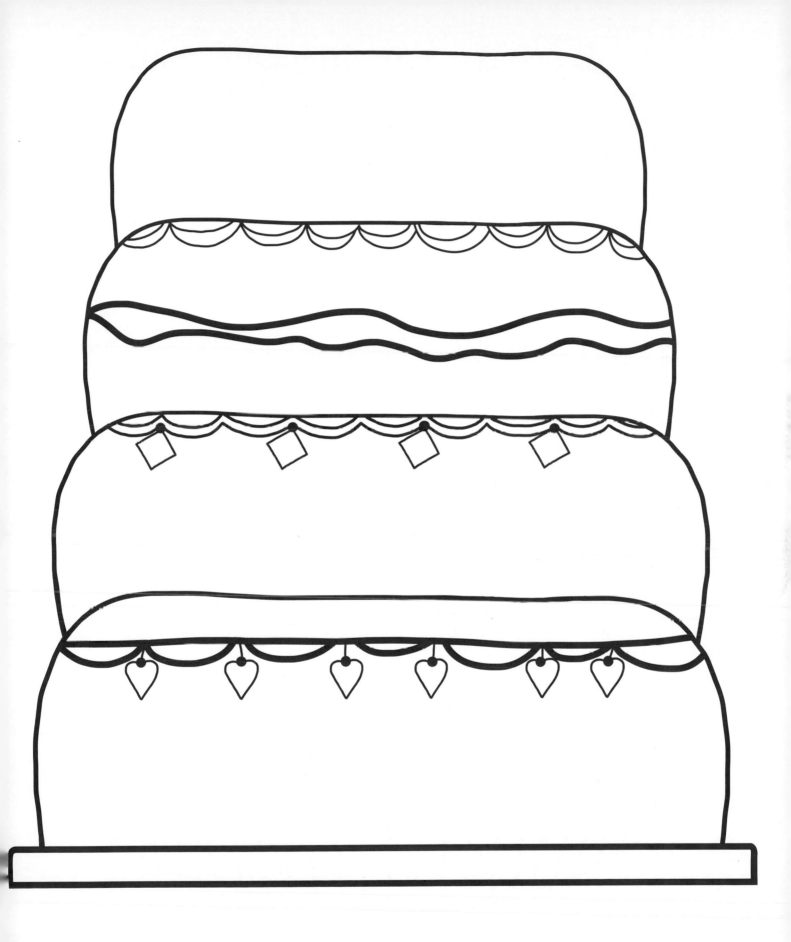

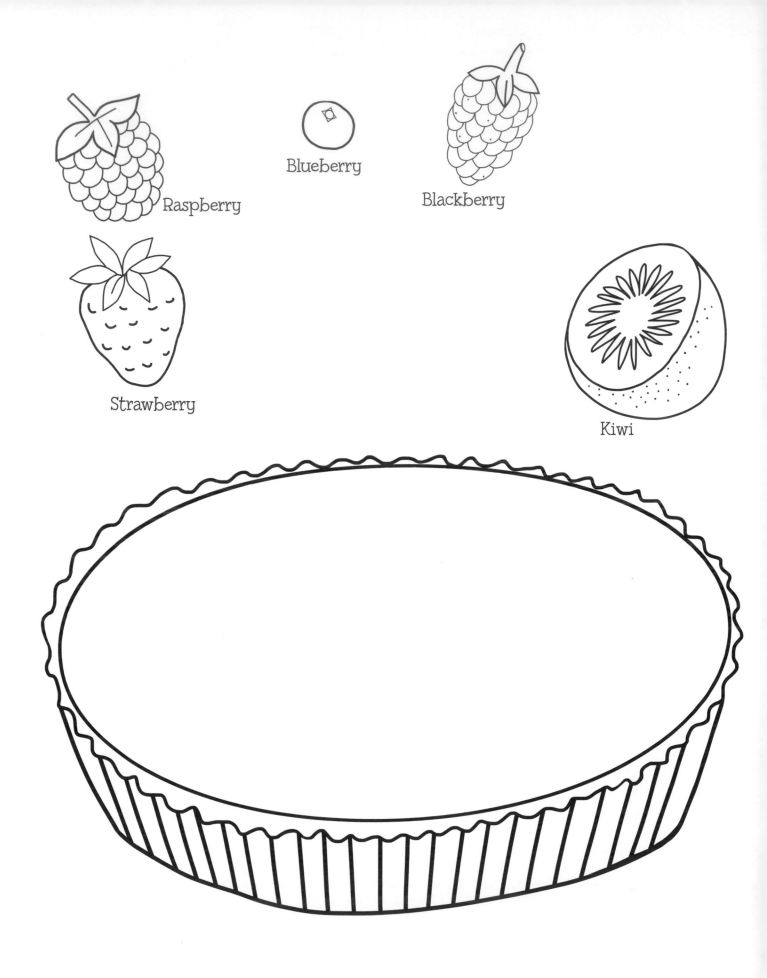

Raspberry

Blueberry

Blackberry

Strawberry

Kiwi

What kind of fruit will go on your fruit tart?

This chef is trying to figure out what to make.
Help her decide by drawing it in her thought bubble!

Connect the dots to see a sweet treat!

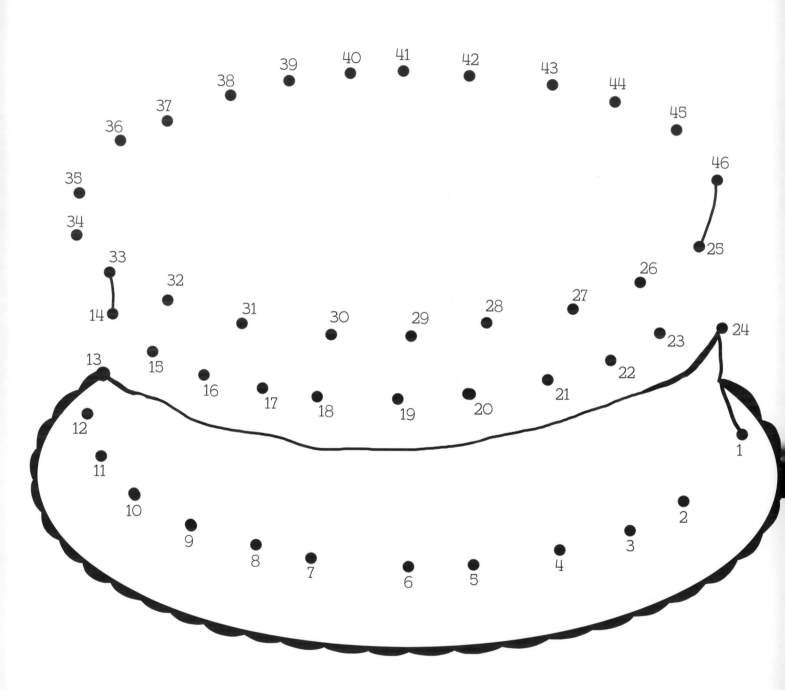

Draw a tasty snack!

Can you spot these images in the scene? Color them in!

Color in these sweet treats!

Decorate these cookies.

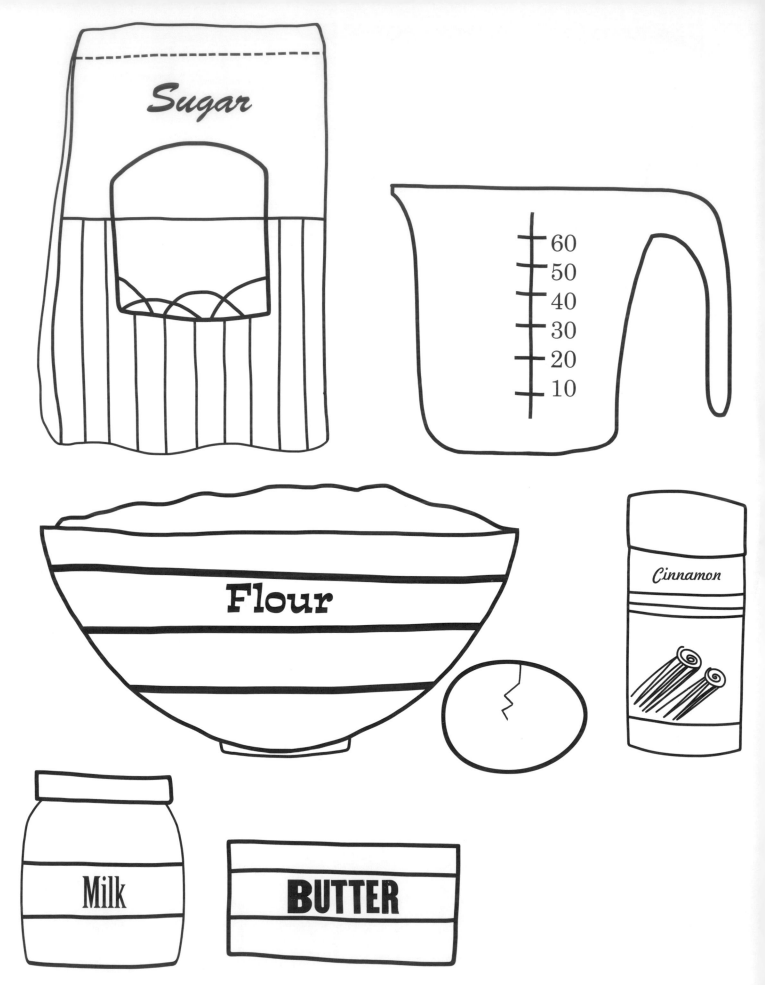

These ingredients are for the treat on the next page. Color them in!

Yum! Can you smell the cinnamon rolls?

Fill this page with all kinds of yummy treats!

Get ready to play dress-up!

These girls are getting ready for a tea party.

Color in their fancy clothes!

These ladies are looking for necklaces
to wear with their ball gowns.
Can you doodle some around their necks?

These kids want to try on cool glasses.
Draw them in!

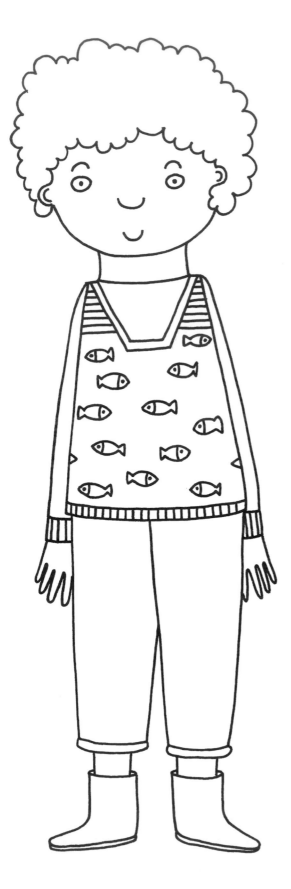

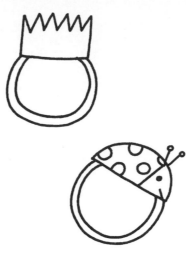

This superhero needs a cape!
Can you pick one for him? Color it in!

Trace the dotted lines to complete this tea set!

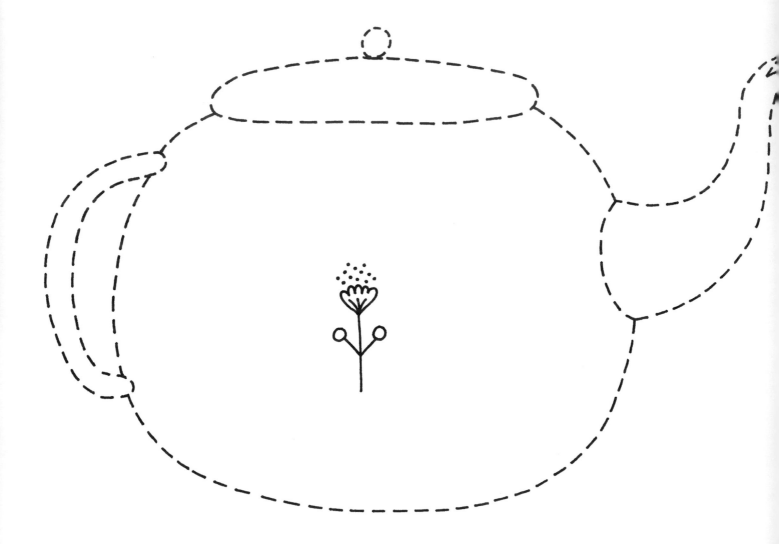

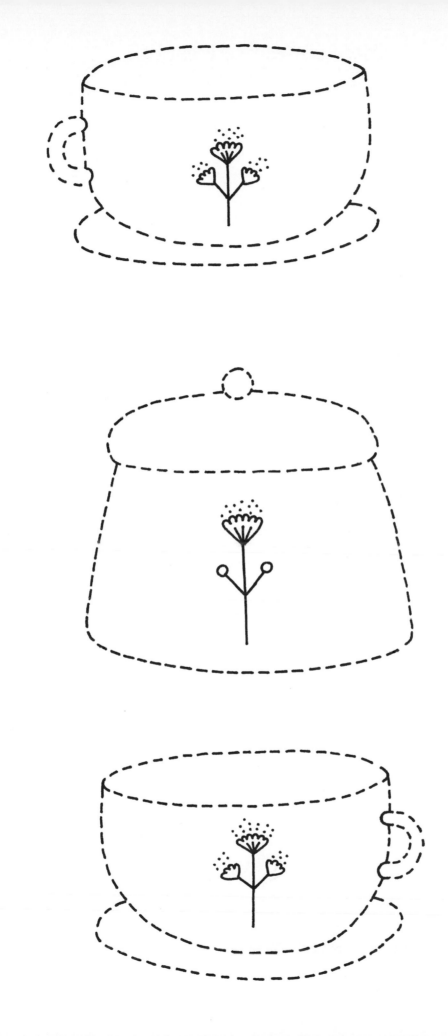

These fairies need wands!

Can you draw some for them?

Look at the two scenes on these pages.
Can you spot the eight differences? Circle them!

Look at all these clothes! If you were going to a fancy dinner party, what would you wear?
Circle the items, and then color them in!

If you could design your own dress, what would it look like?
Draw it for everyone to see!

Now draw a pair of shoes to go with it!

Trace the dotted lines to complete these great outfits!

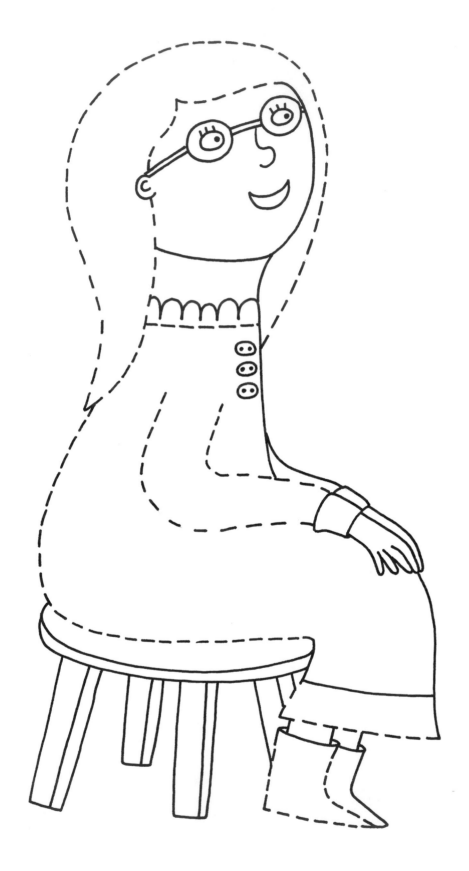

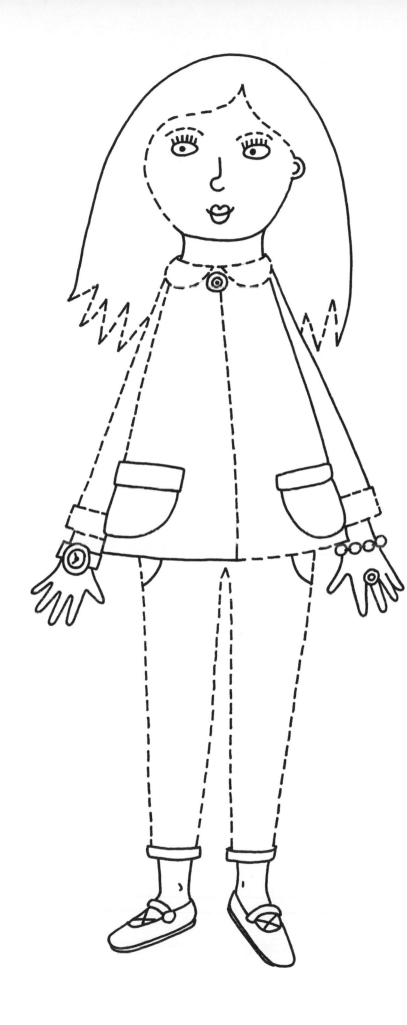

Look at all these beautiful bracelets!
Can you find the two that are exactly alike? Circle them!

Draw some fun feather boas around these ladies' necks!

Two of these gentlemen are missing their moustaches.
Draw them in!

Decorate these toenails! Use stars, hearts,
stripes—or anything you like!

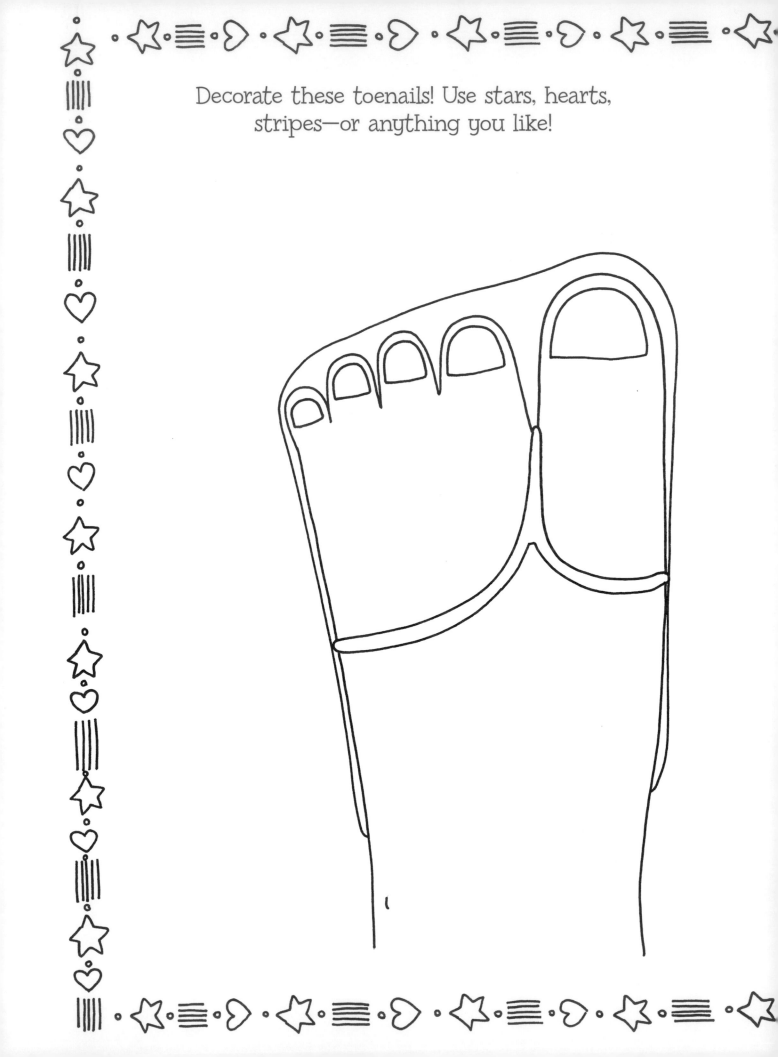

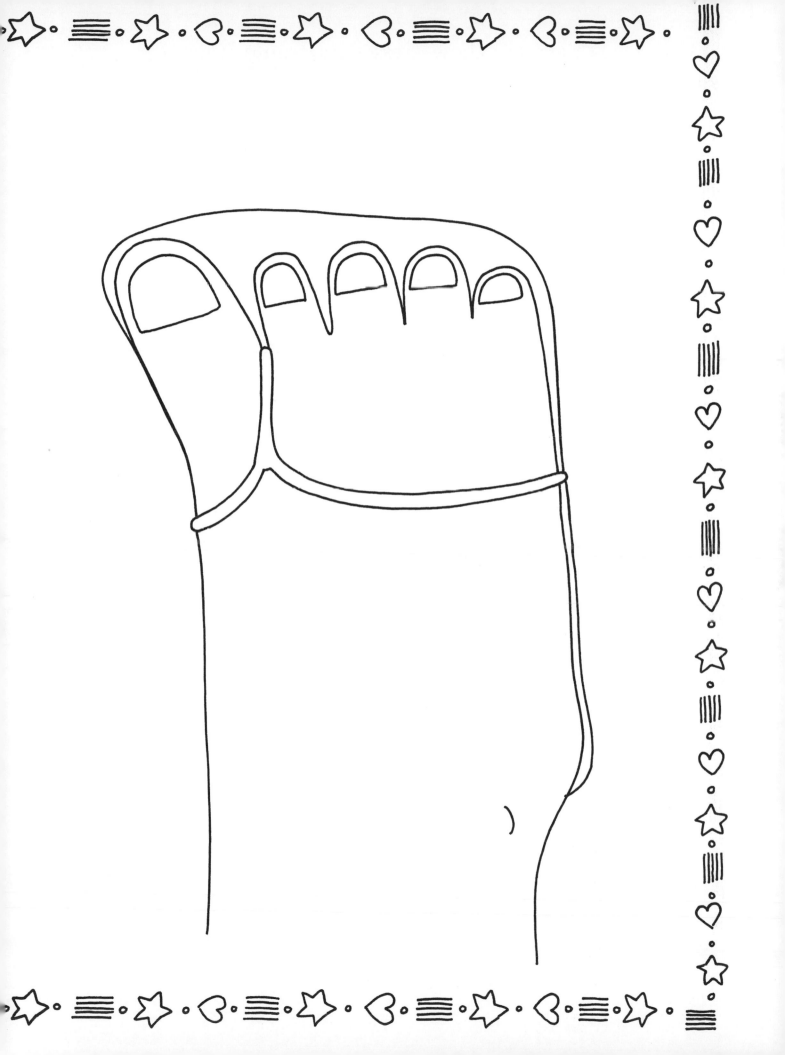

Decorate these dresses any way you like!

Add some unique hairstyles to these people!

There are five crowns hidden in this scene.
Can you find them?
Color them in!

These men need bow ties. Doodle some in!

Can you put the finishing touches on this scene?
Hint: Add in pirate hats, eye patches, and swords.

Now color in the scene!

Oh no! It's raining!
Add some umbrellas to the scene to keep the bumblebee
and ladybug dry.

Color in these scarves!

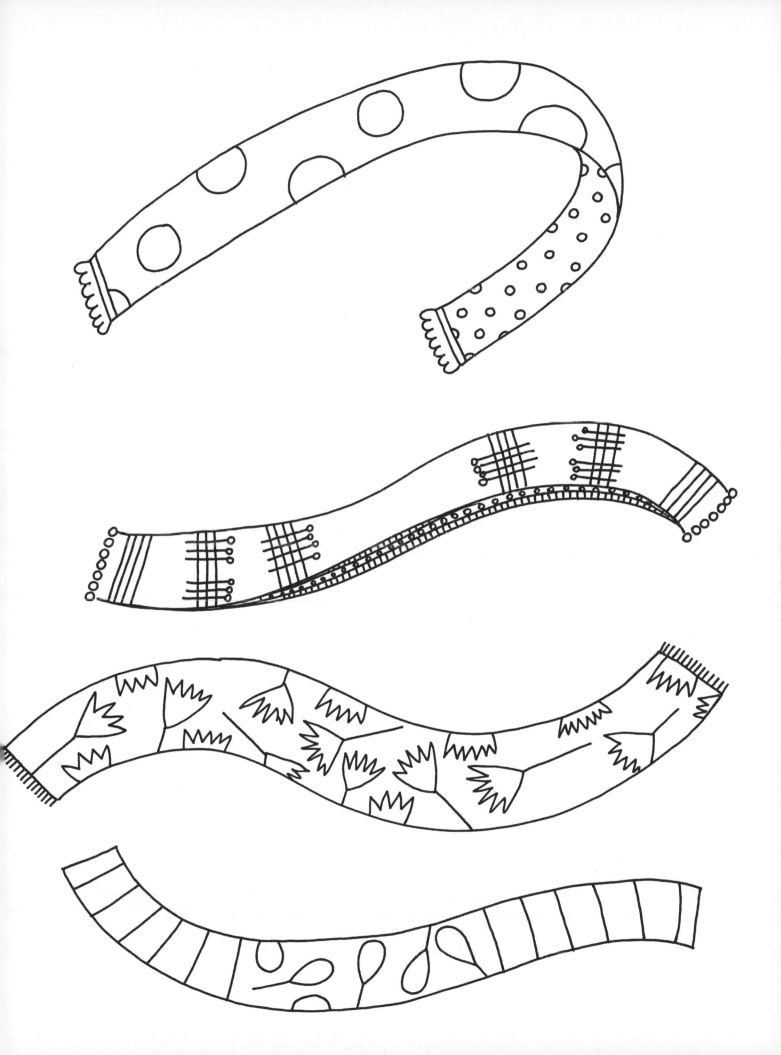

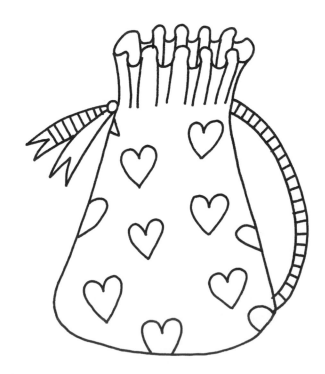

Which bag is your favorite? Color it in!

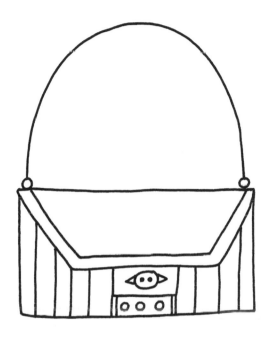

Now color in the rest!

Connect the dots to create some stockings.

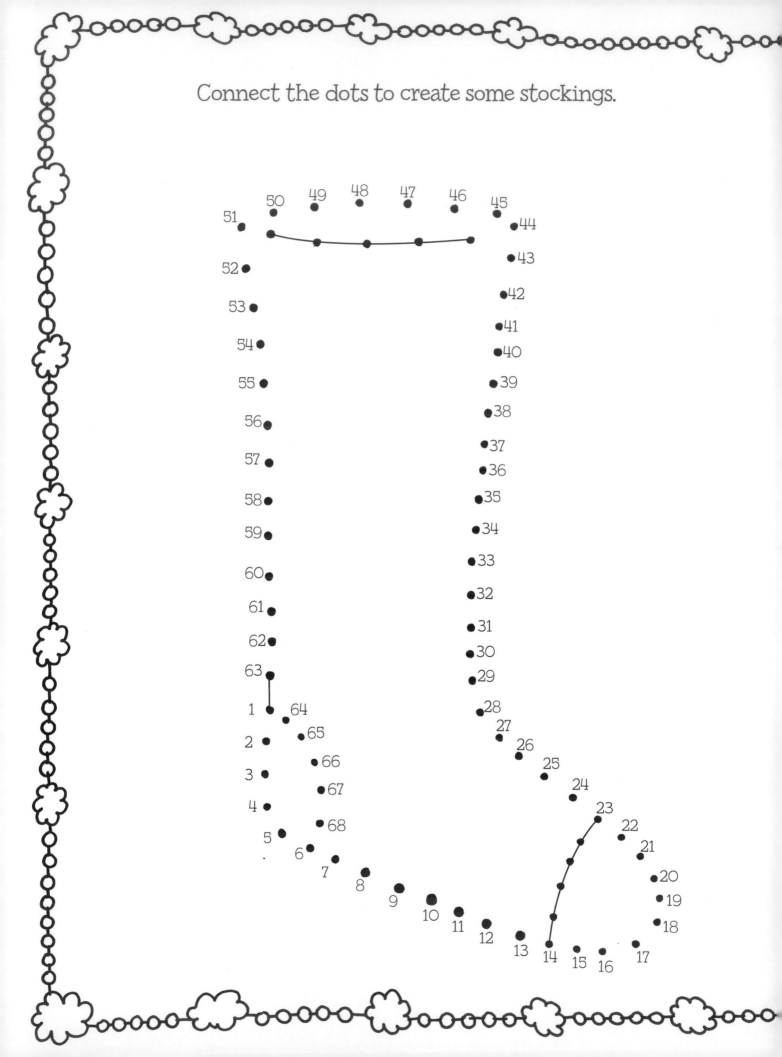

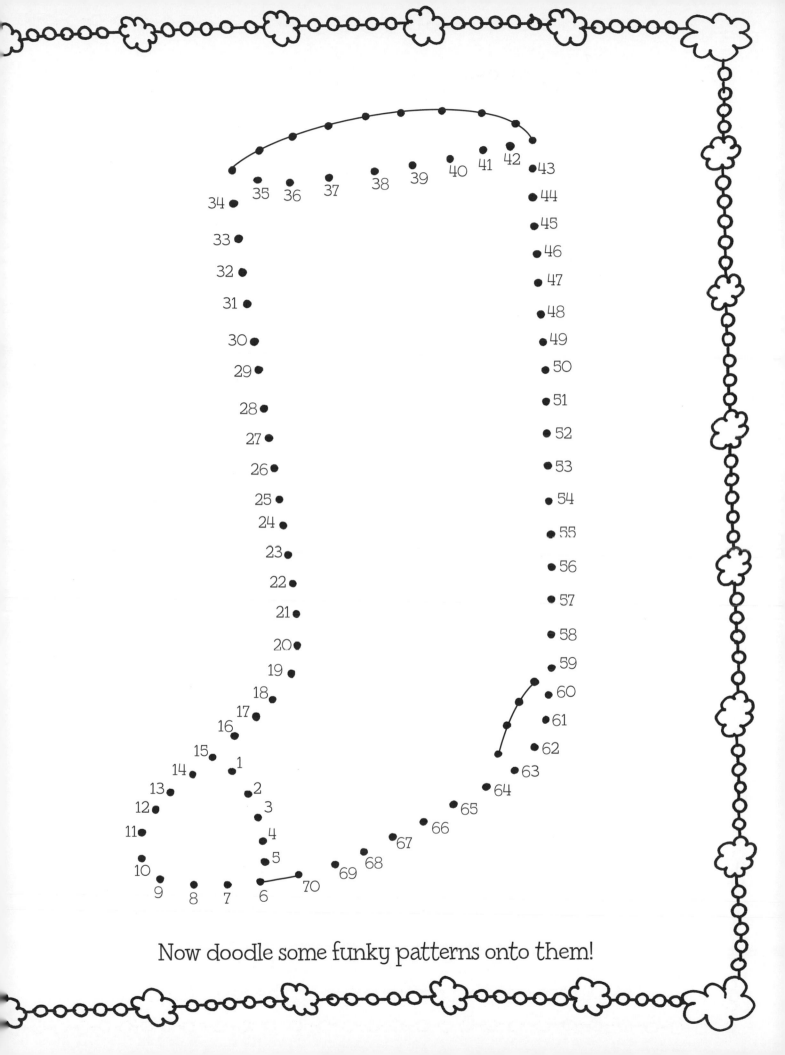

Now doodle some funky patterns onto them!

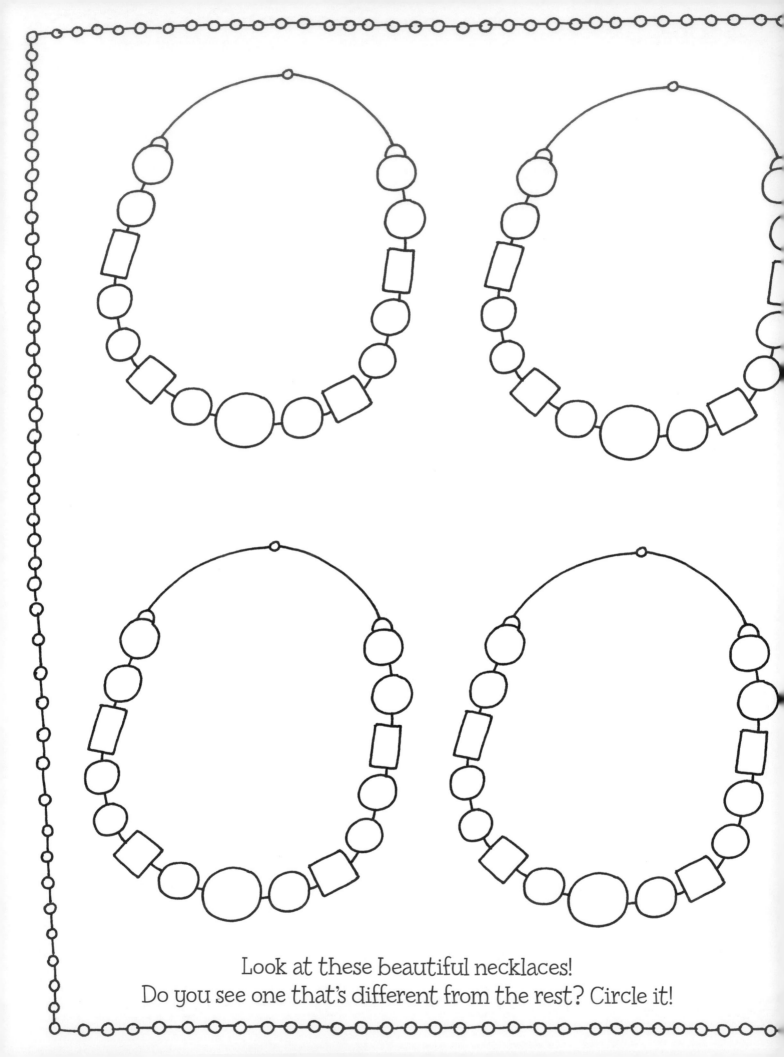

Look at these beautiful necklaces!
Do you see one that's different from the rest? Circle it!

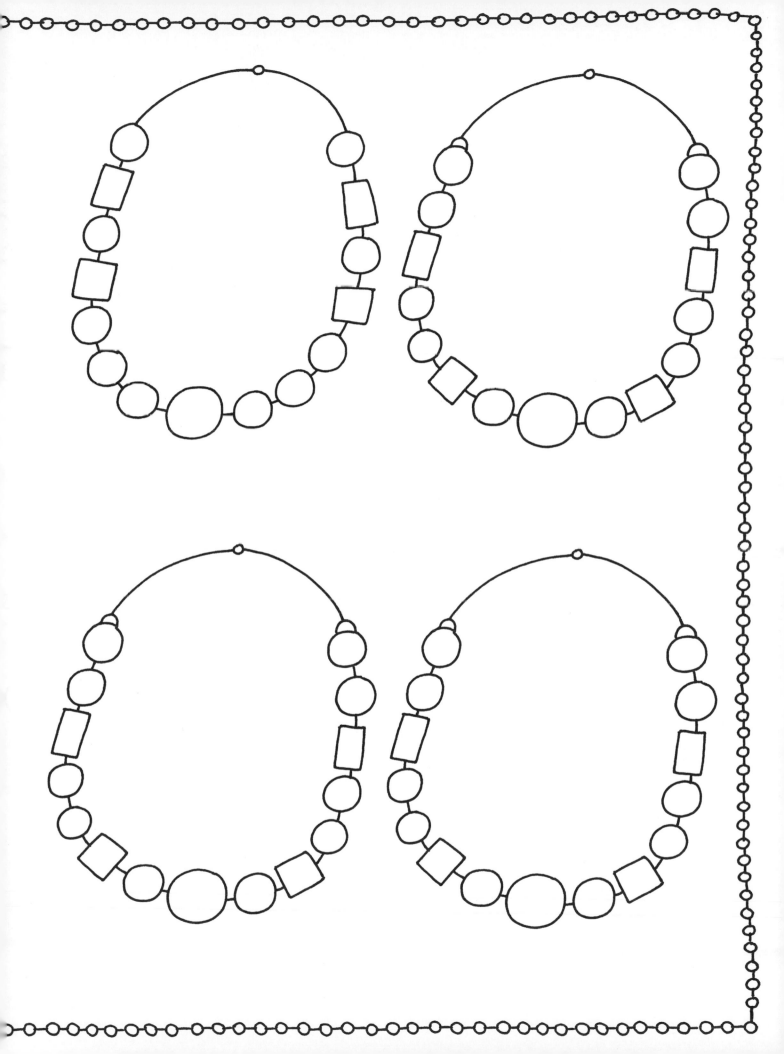

A little girl has lost her ring.
Can you help her find it?

Start

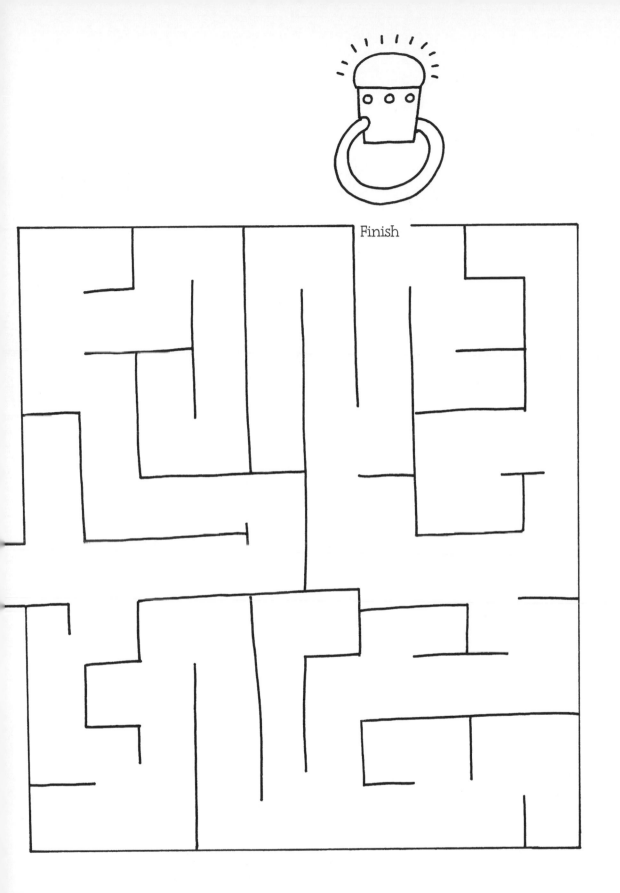

Finish

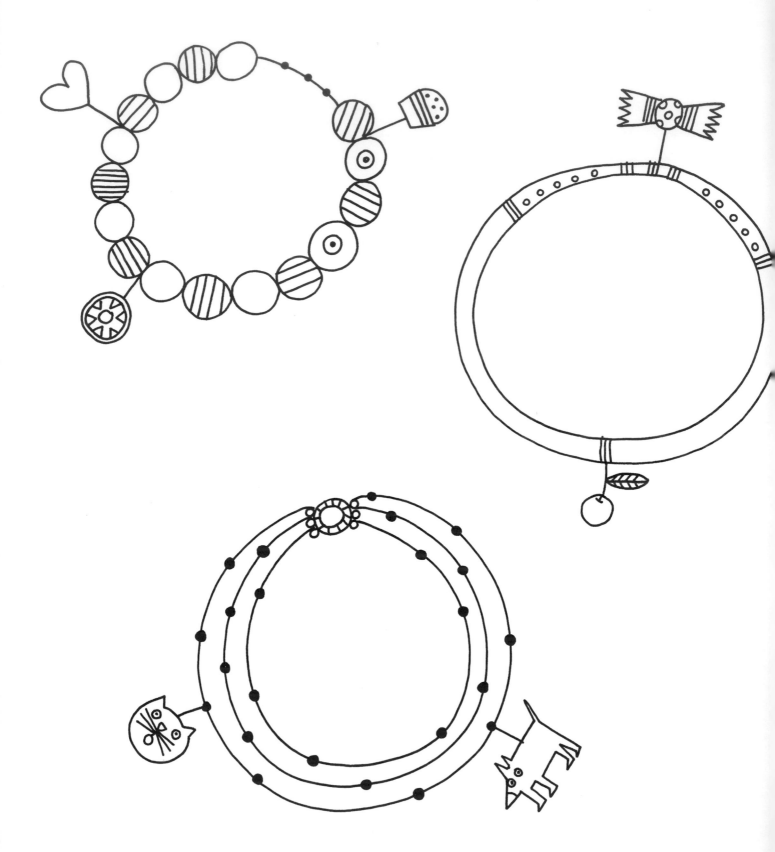

What pretty charm bracelets!
Can you add some more charms to them?

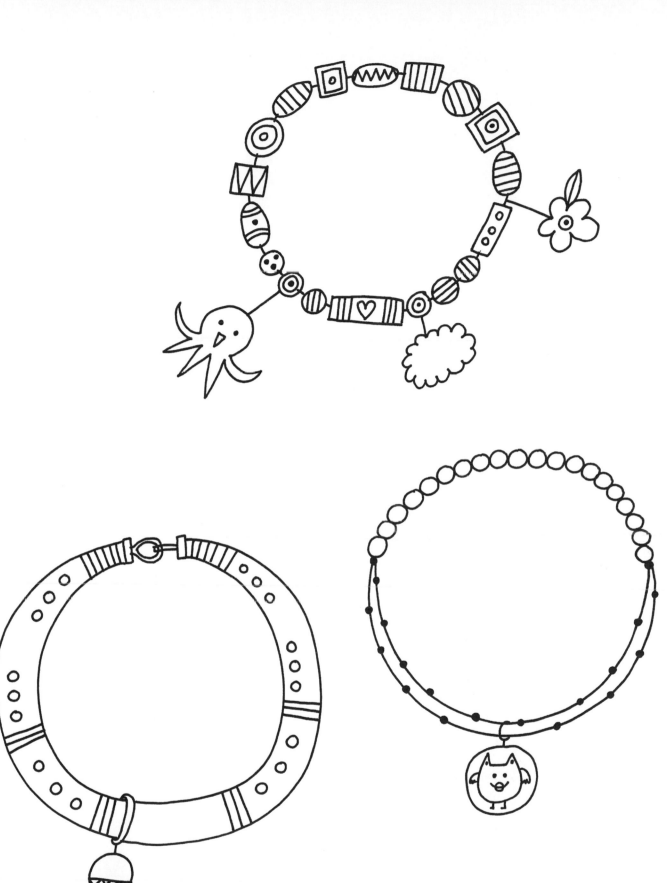

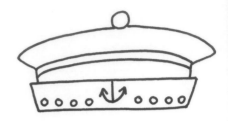

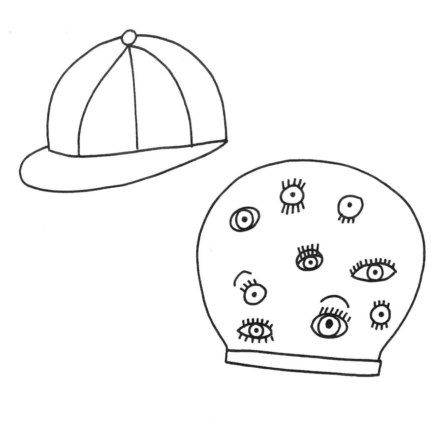

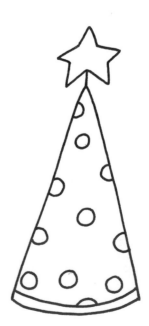
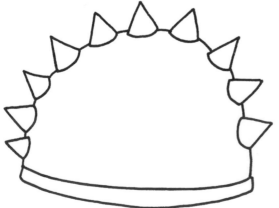

Draw some fun hats onto these ladies' heads.

These girls want to be ballerinas.
Can you give them some tutus?

Now color in the scene!

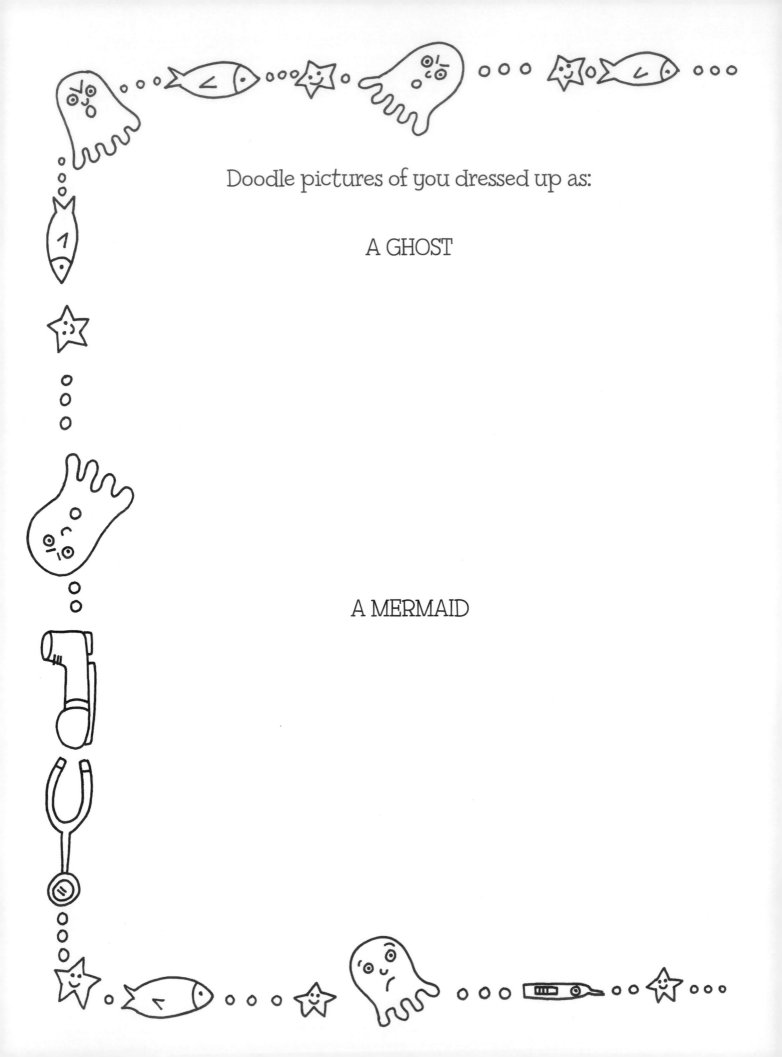

Doodle pictures of you dressed up as:

A GHOST

A MERMAID

A CLOWN

A DOCTOR

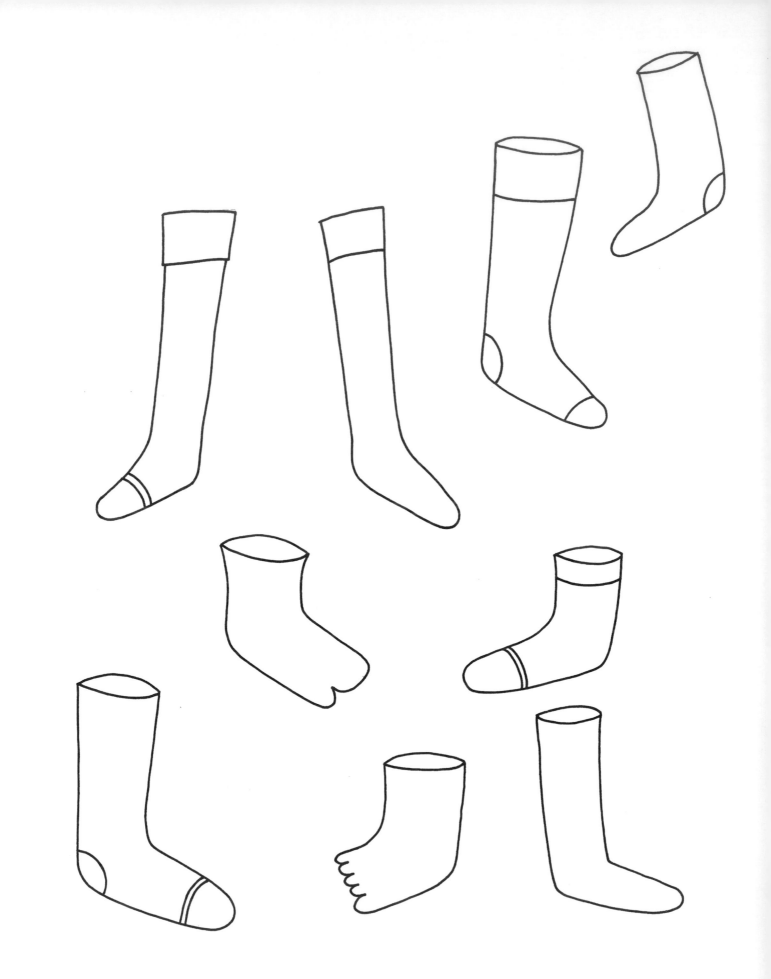

Decorate these socks with your favorite patterns!

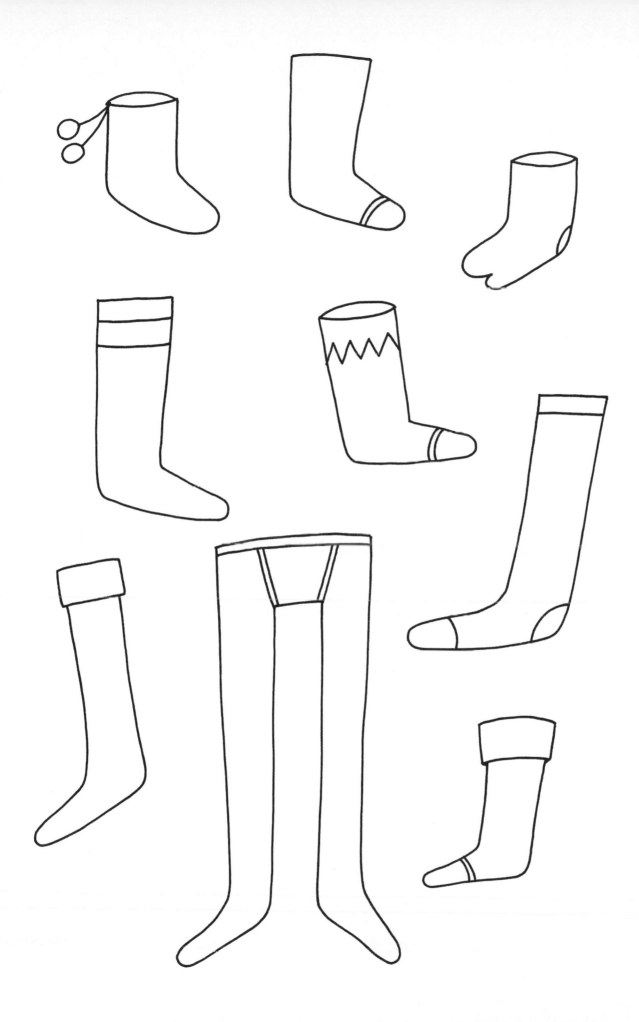

These kids have dressed up as pastry chefs.
Decorate their aprons any way you like!

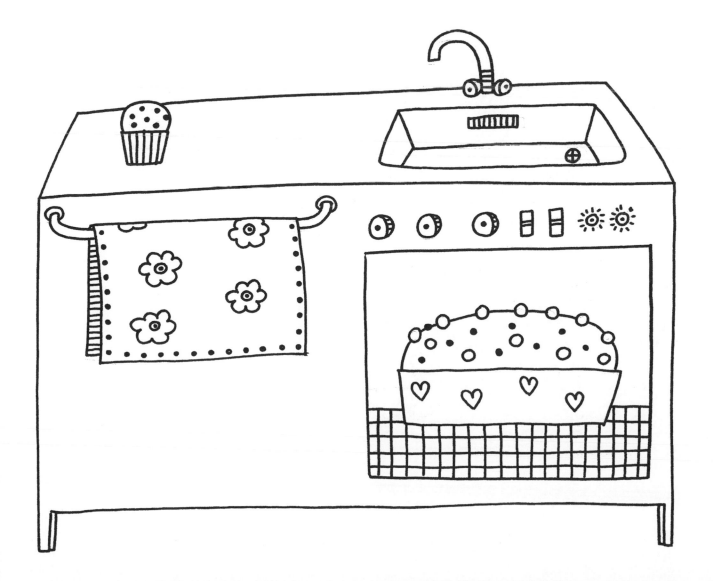

This cowboy and cowgirl can't find their hats.
Can you doodle some on them?

Now color in the scene!

Can you spot these images?
Color them in!

Color in these paper dolls any way you like!

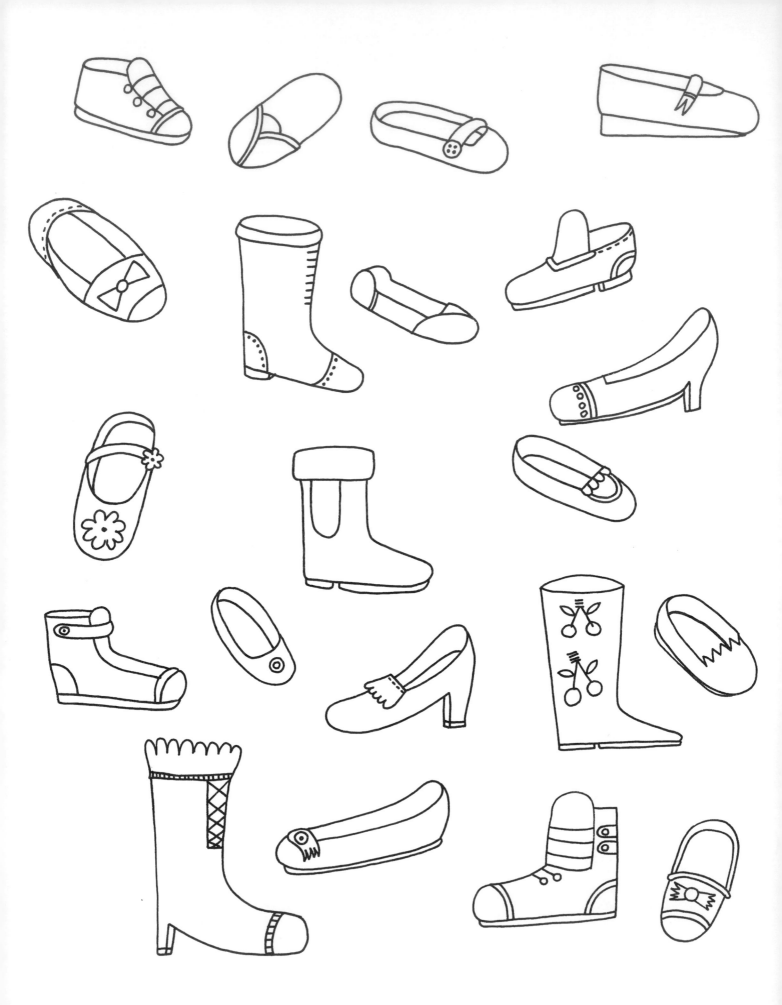

Can you find the six hats that look exactly like this one?
Circle them, and then color them in!

Yikes—a dragon!
Trace the dotted lines to create a knight that will scare it away!

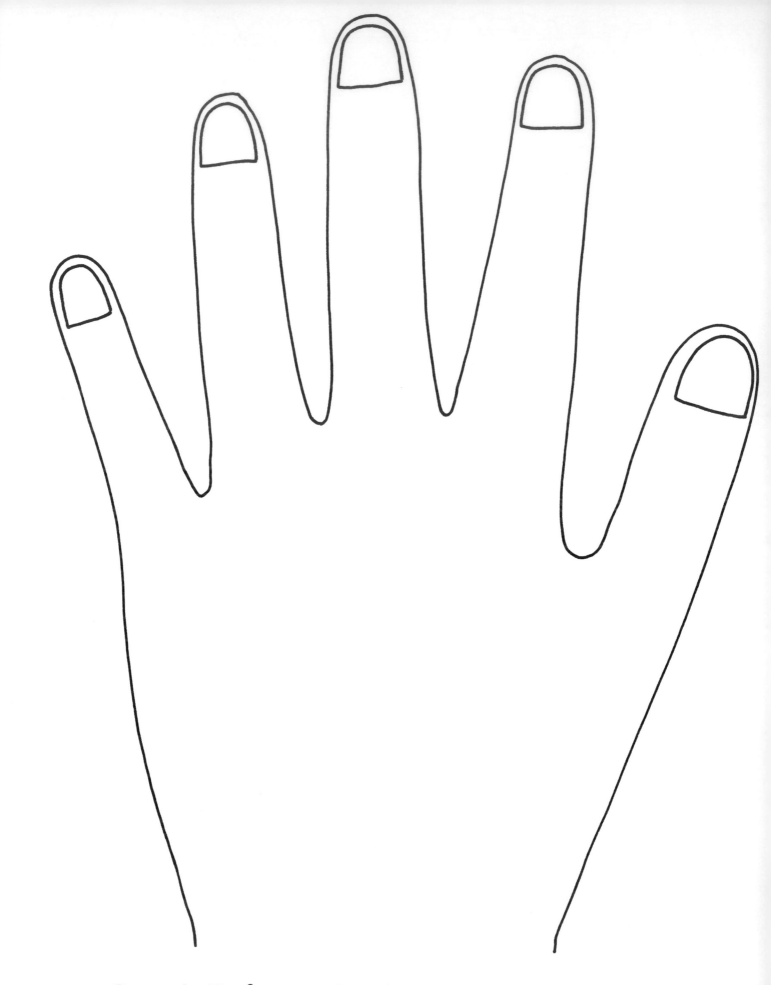

Decorate the fingernails on these hands any way you like!

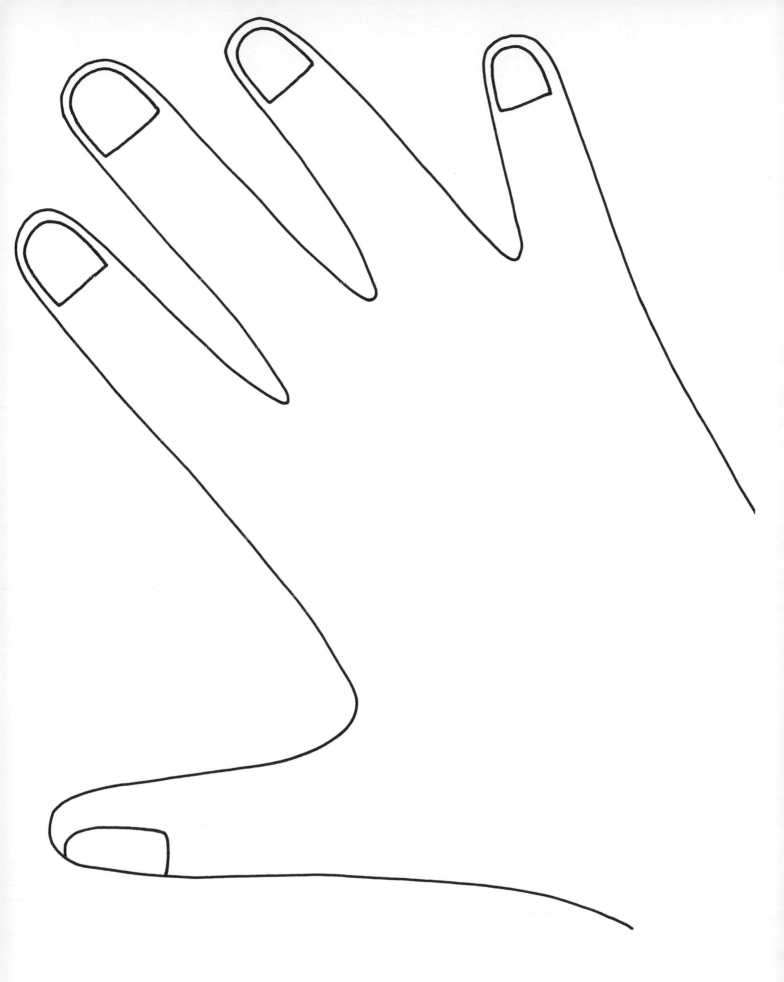

Then draw some rings on them!

This princess has lost her glass slipper!
Help her find it—and her prince!

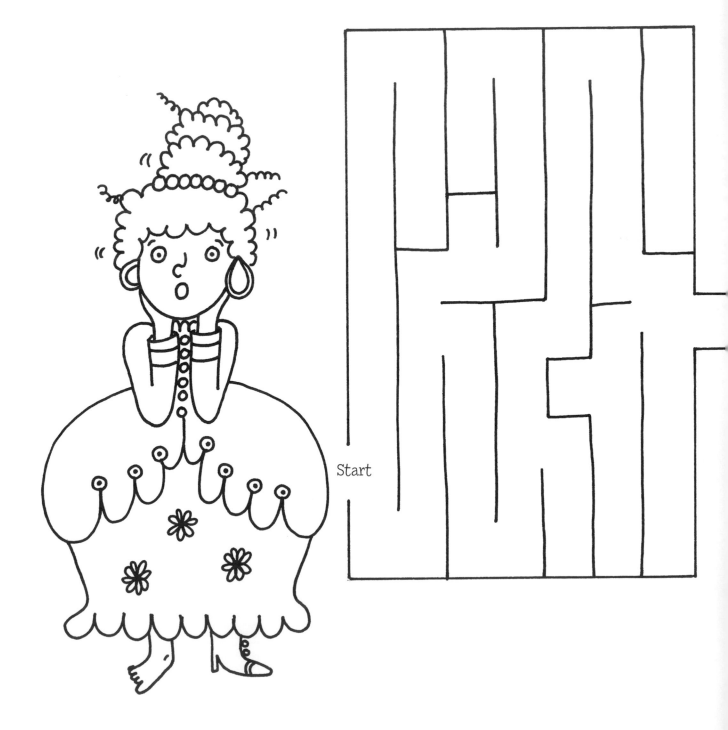

Start

Finish

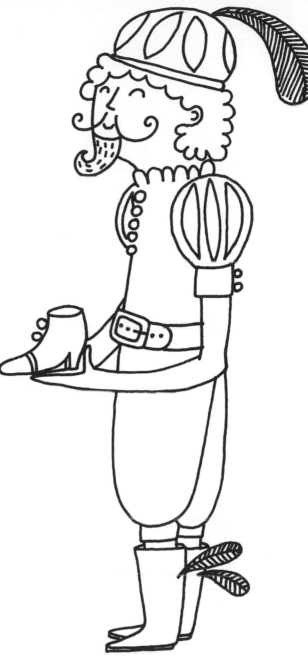

These kids want to go outside and play in the snow.
What clothes should they wear? Color them in!

Look at this growing garden!
Color it in.

These bees smell some pretty flowers.

Can you spot all eight ants in this scene?
Circle them!

Some seeds were just planted.
Draw what they grow into!

Color in this scene. Then turn the page to find out
what's going on underground!

Color in this
fancy garden.

This bird needs to get back to his nest. Can you help him?

Start

Finish

These are some of the insects you might find in the garden.
Color them in!

Decorate and color these gardening gloves.

Now decorate and color these sun hats.

Connect the dots to see what's growing in the garden.

Hissssss . . .

Who. Who.

Chirp! Chirp!

Buzzzzz . . .

Connect the animal or insect to the sound it makes!

These are some of the flowers you might find in the garden.
Color them in!

Decorate this vase and add some flowers to it.

Let's get silly. Draw some sunglasses on these critters!

These birds need a place to perch.
Draw some branches on this tree.

Which of these is perfect to use in a delicious cake? Circle it.

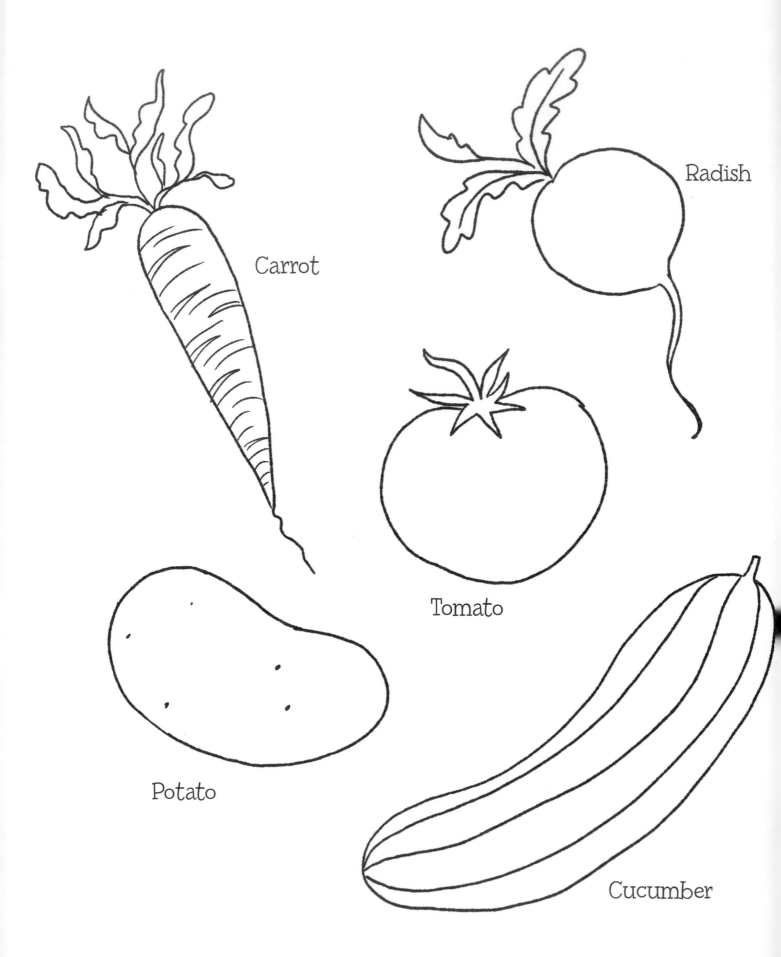

Carrot

Radish

Tomato

Potato

Cucumber

Yum! A carrot cake!

Which two bunny rabbits are exactly alike?

What is this chipmunk thinking about? Draw it in his thought bubble.

Doodle some designs on these pinwheels.

This is the toolshed. Color in the tools.

This fruit needs some color! Can you color the apples green,
the blueberries blue, the grapes purple, and the strawberries red?

A garden needs sunlight! Draw a sun in the sky.

Decorate the wings of these butterflies.

This watering can must water the flowers. Can you help it get to them?

Start

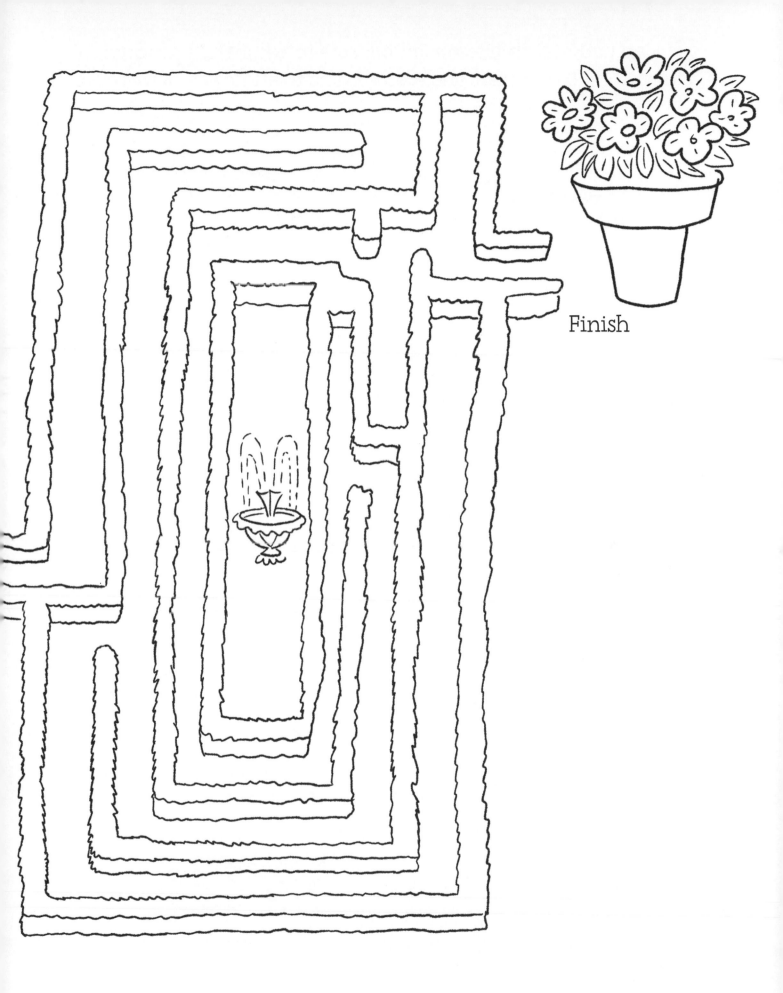

Finish

Can you match these seed packets to what they produce?
Draw a line to connect the seeds to the fruit, flower, or vegetable.

It's raining! The water is good for the garden.
Draw the rain falling from the clouds.

Color in this field of sunflowers.

These caterpillars are about to turn into beautiful butterflies.

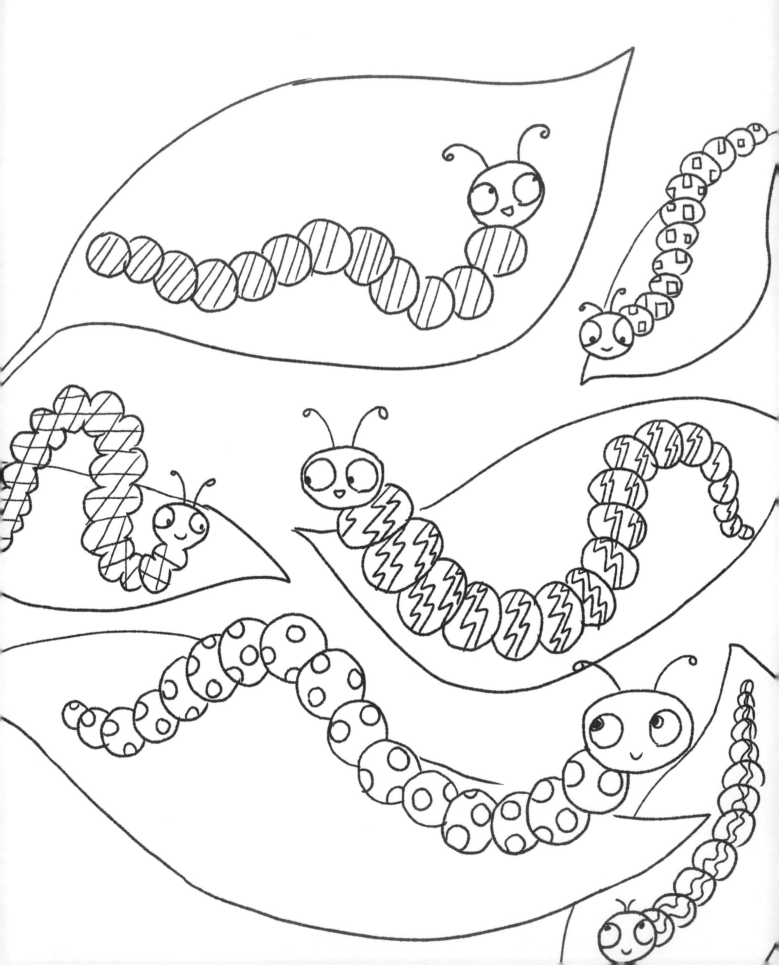

The caterpillars have turned into butterflies! Color them in.

Can you spot the eight ladybugs in this scene?

Color in the plants and animals according to the color that's listed by each one.

Blue

Pink

Orange

Purple

Yellow

Green

Red

Can you draw some silly hats and jewelry on these ants?

These plants are thirsty.
Draw water coming out of the watering can!

Topiaries are bushes that are trimmed into shapes!
On the line below each topiary, write what it's in the shape of.

Some foods grow in the ground. Color them in!

Some foods grow on vines. Color them in!

Who's peeking out of the holes in this tree?
Draw them!

Doodle some fun designs on these snails' shells.

Color these lettuce plants different shades of green.

Draw the other half of this tree!

Can you spot these images in the scene?

These are some of the tools you would use in a garden.

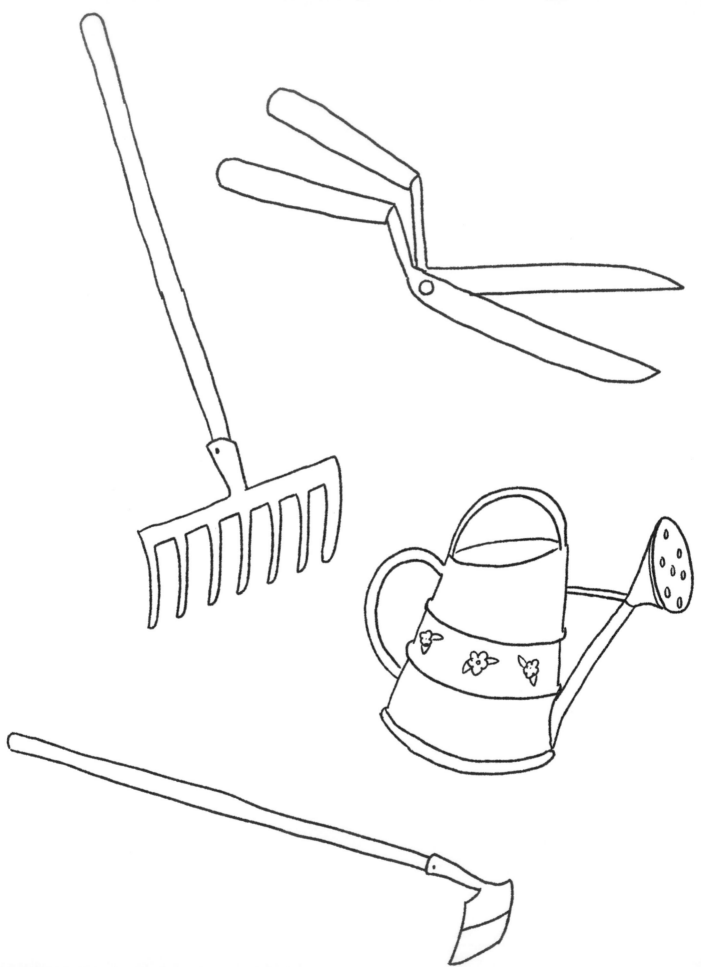

Let's have some fun! Decorate these vegetables with
wacky stripes and polka dots.

Now do the same for this fruit!

On the tags, label each plant, vegetable, and flower in this garden.

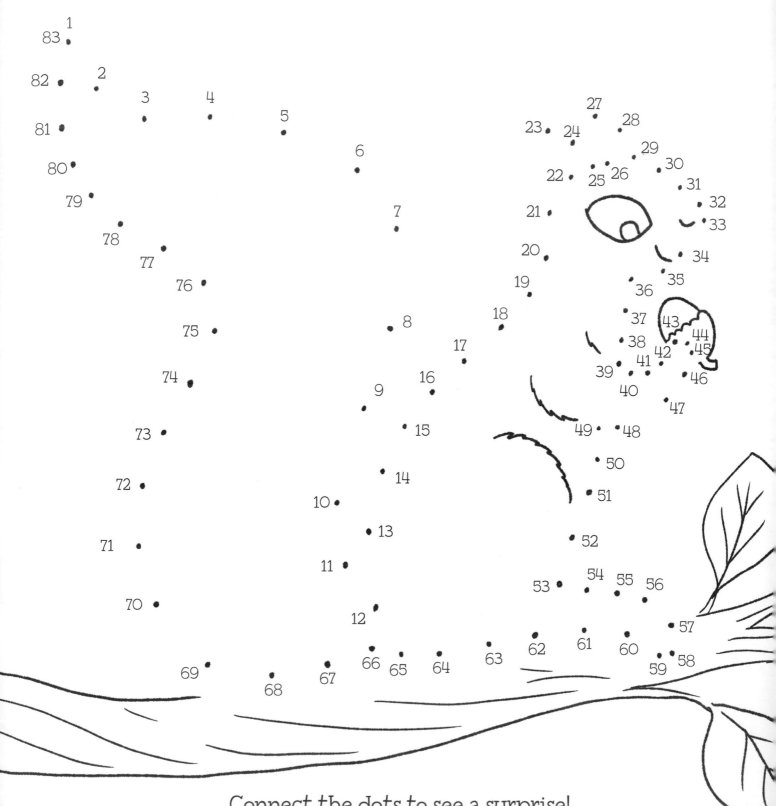

Connect the dots to see a surprise!

These flowers are about to bloom. Draw petals around their buds!

What does this squirrel see outside of its tree burrow?

Look at all these plants. Can you find the two that are exactly alike?

Draw your favorite flower here!

This family of chipmunks is looking for some lunch.

What do you think they want to eat? Draw it here!

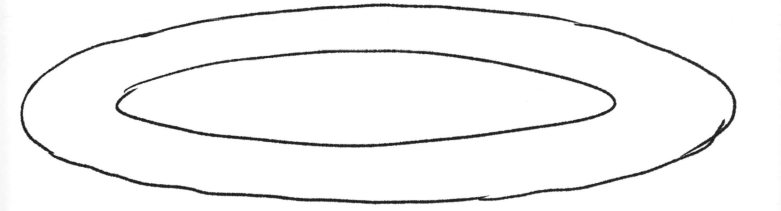

Fill these pages with a garden of your own.
Draw bugs, flowers, vegetables, and fruit!

This bunny is dreaming about something. Draw it in her thought bubble.

Draw some silly googly eyes
on these caterpillars.

Can you spot these images in the scene?

Can you complete the fence around this garden to keep the deer out?

Decorate these pots any way you want!

Color in this scene!

Start

These ants have to get home.
Can you help them?

Finish

Look at all these dragonflies.
Can you find the two that are exactly alike? Circle them!

What's in each of these nests? Draw it!

Color in this beautiful bouquet of flowers.